I0619913

IT CAME FROM SPACE

EDDIE GENEROUS

SEVERED PRESS
HOBART TASMANIA

IT CAME FROM SPACE

Copyright © 2021 EDDIE GENEROUS

WWW.SEVEREDPRESS.COM

ISBN: 978-1-922551-98-6

1

The sun had gone to an almost blinding white for the last nineteen minutes, though none of the local fauna had evolved to a state where counting time was achievable. Treetops several hundred feet into the sky began to blacken and the needles and leaves began to sizzle and dry, raining down in a diming grey ash. Far below, on the lip of a swampy pond, a beast not so different from Earth's Purussaurus of the Neogene Period—still one hundred billion years from existence and two solar systems away—slipped into the murky water, looking for a reprieve from the sudden heat. Ravenous, it pushed to the silty bottom and dragged its three-meter-long lower jaw along the bed, scooping fish-like creatures and crab-like creatures in a mouthful before snapping shut and working its rough tongue like a sushi mixer. It swallowed the same moment a great ripple played into the pond from above.

Everything began to shake, enough so that the water was shimmying. The heat from below began to rise and a red core opened and sucked the pond from beneath while replacing the displaced water with rising steam. The beast raced toward the top and all the blackness above. Seeing by feel, it hit the surf and leapt, pushing its incredible forelegs like a spring to reach the lagoon fifteen feet away. The waterway attaching the pond and the lagoon had already dried, but the beast didn't know that, it only knew it had to get away from the molten heat rising from below.

The landing following the leap was hard and heavy; more than half the water in the lagoon had evaporated and took with it the softening silt and flora that had grown atop the thick rock base. Shaking, scared, and unused to the sensation, the beast stayed afloat, unwilling to sink or rise. Hours passed and then days. The planet was shaking still, but the water had cooled from above. The sun was gone. Exploded. It had sent a great ball of plasma into a volcano not far from where the beast had spent her entire life. The plasma had burned through to the center of the planet and rotated upon gravity's pull, spinning, spreading heat, reacting to the metals hidden within the soil. Up top, with the local sun obliterated, the world quickly cooled until freezing.

The beast could remain below the surf for more than a day without coming up for air and pulled as long stretches as it could below in the unknown. The water around it had gone chunky and grey while it slept. The beast attempted to break through to the top for air. It couldn't and grew frantic, wriggling and trying to chomp, before stopping at a fresh crack and drinking in the life-giving oxygen. It remained there until it froze solid and icy rains patched the cracks, sealing it in a glass coffin.

Below the crust of the lagoon, through miles upon miles of solid stone, the ball of plasma and swirling metals had reached the point of calamity and instability. The ball burst outward and shattered the world, sending a massive chunk of ice hurtling through the black, black universe, catching speeds unachievable in gravity-based situations. Catching speeds dangerously hard to fathom.

The ice ball grew steadily, collecting debris and particles from the endless dance of expansion and existence. The high-speed ball managed to miss anything detrimental for just shy of one hundred billion years. It snapped in half upon colliding with an asteroid, sending it toward Earth's solar system. It nudged and bumped three more times in the following three hundred thousand years and was about to miss Earth completely when it struck an orphaned Chinese satellite that had drifted from orbit. Another half broke away from the icy rock that was now hurtling toward the Pacific Northwest of North America.

When it entered Earth's atmosphere, the collected debris almost instantly vaporized. The ice followed suit. The beast was almost bare. Its scaly armor began to burn and for nine seconds, its heart began to beat anew before ceasing for a final time. It continued its crash, that thick leather armor deteriorating, but withstanding enough that the beast maintained her shape, maintained her innards.

The beast slammed into the Pacific Ocean only thirty miles from the remote fishing and tourism community on Picture Island. Somewhere, hundreds of miles away, the impact was registered, but concerned no one beyond one curious astronomer who had a bucket list with this one particular item on it—given where it had landed, it would be nearly impossible to locate and would have only the slimmest of chances of harming any of the local populations: plant or animal. Fishing boats not far felt a wave on the foggy morning but had no clue otherwise.

The beast's corpse slammed into a rock shelf only feet below the surf and its armor cracked and broke away in pieces, taking with them shattered bones and chunks of charred meat as the steam bubbles rose in a frantic race to the surface of the water. In seconds, all that remained was a quickly thawing womb and twenty feet of baby beast about to take its first breaths without its mother's help. Just as soon as it cracked its egg and uncoiled its powerful form.

2

Carole McNaughton gazed out at the rippling blue of the ocean waters, hoping to see a whale but content to simply be away from home and work, and breathe in the open air. As a new mother and recent widow, she felt she deserved a vacation, even one where the destination was familiar as the indestructible pair of Express Jeans she'd had since her first year of college. Amazing that a pair of $40 jeans could outlast a loving marriage. More amazing that she hadn't seen the end coming.

Unlike the jeans, the fabric of her husband had been flawed from the beginning. Shane had tried to be a self-sustaining writer, had sold books to small presses and short stories to even smaller presses. He'd been officially unemployed for five years and from the beginning gave himself a six-year window to get good enough to sell something of note—the same time it would likely have taken him to go the official, expensive route of acquiring an MFA. His work had become his life and the more he explored his existence, mining for stories, the easier it became to see that the chances of anything working out were slim, which meant he'd have to focus and dig, find a way around his genre's gatekeepers rather than through them. Part of his introspection had led him to a crossroads with Carole. She wanted a baby and he calmly told her he'd kill himself if she ever got pregnant. It was the kind of sentiment that didn't play well with most and Carole didn't take it seriously—she didn't take much of what he did all that seriously.

Nowadays, she made great money and he made good supper.

The call had come on a dreary, rainy day, but one no different from any other day, and her knees buckled. Her in-laws had died in a car accident and their two children needed guardians—the only other options lived out of the country. Carole's own mother offered, but she was sixty-two and lived in the woods up in the hills on Picture Island; plus, she had no connection to the children and they'd never even met her, so that wouldn't work. Carole's husband Shane wasn't overly troubled by the news of his brother's death—they exchanged annual Christmas cards and that was the extent of it—but that Carole wanted the children made him gaze off into space. Carole didn't have to discuss, not really, she made the money and the rules without it ever being put so plainly. Shane didn't complain. He put his work on hold—it never even crossed Carole's mind to put her own work on hold—and dealt with the changes for a total of nine weeks. He grew more somber in that time, hardly wrote and seemed only vaguely aware of his inbox—before that, the inbox was his lifeline, his only hope for tomorrows to come.

Carole awoke on a Sunday morning to find Shane's side of the bed empty and cold. She thought little of it and went to check his office. He was sporadic and had been diligent before the kids. He put down words whenever they came and pushed himself when the words weren't there waiting on his fingertips. But his office was empty. She went to the kitchen to find the coffeemaker off and nothing having been brewed since the day before. No other interior options, she stepped through the back door and looked out on the subdivision from her stubby porch. The birds sang and a gentle breeze blew sand across the fresh black asphalt. Across the lot, one of the neighbors was hooking a kayak to the roof of his SUV.

Not dressed and not wanting to be seen, Carole turned back, noticing only then that the garage light was on. Back inside and into the kitchen, she opened the door to the garage and drank in the scene. Her ever considerate husband had put painting plastic on the floor beneath him to catch any of the fluids that would drain from his hung corpse where it swayed on a red and black electrical cord. On his chest was a piece of paper that read I'M NO DAD.

Pain hitched and she wanted to scream that just because his parents were trash, it didn't mean he couldn't be better. Just because kids ate up his free time didn't mean he couldn't chase a lofty goal. Just because he never wanted this in his life, it didn't mean he couldn't do it for her. But she didn't, because finally, in that moment while her husband of ten years swayed a dozen inches from the floor, she understood that she'd never considered it from his side. She'd always seen it as something she could manipulate, something to needle into place. Hadn't she needled a million things just right countless times before? She had never for a second actually considered that he simply wanted to exist without fully going through the never-ending cycle of the human race: birth, pro-creation, death.

Carole fell to her knees and cried until she heard the kids moving around within the house. She rose then and wiped her face, catching another epiphany: she knew she was sacrificing at least the marriage to take these children in, she knew she was sacrificing the marriage every time she'd secretly gone off the pill, she knew and should've at least had an inkling that this might happen—*he told you, remember?* She had wanted babies, but an eight-year-old girl and an eleven-year-old boy would do for now.

The kids were shocked by the revelation, but it wasn't as if Carole was sadistic, she hadn't shown them the note, had only shown one old beat cop the note—he unpinned it and let her throw it away before anyone came to collect the body.

And now here they were, Alexis playing with two other little girls and George reading one of Shane's old *The House of Mystery* comics, while they rode a twenty-car passenger boat, off to see Grandma. The total trip one-way was more than three hours, with most of that occurring on the ocean.

Carole turned from the rusty white railing and said, "You guys hungry?"

Alexis instantly forgot her new friends and b-lined, doped to the gills on soda and Twizzlers.

"Can I have chicken fingers and ketchup?"

George looked up from the PG horrors of the comic and tilted his head, as if saying that chicken fingers was an idea all right.

The small restaurant in the ship had a fryer and by the smell of most of the cabin, chicken fingers and fries were an option. Carole never ate on the boat when she went across, not on any of the dozen or so trips she'd made since her mother left the mainland seven years earlier. The food was trashy and overpriced, but something had clicked since the kids had been around and she was coming to appreciate many of the things she herself had enjoyed in youth all over again.

"We can have chicken fingers, but only if we can have ice cream after," Carole said. She was in a giving mood, something that happened whenever she let herself think deeply about Shane.

George slapped closed the comic on his lap and nodded once while Alexis began fist-pumping at her side like she'd just roofed a slapshot past a goalie.

3

The official stance on Picture Island was that it had been uninhabited in the year 1811 when ten fishermen and their families escaping civilization had settled there. Six of those men died within four months. Three women died within three months. Twelve children died in their first two months of life on the island.

It hadn't been uninhabited, not quite, not in a sense that nobody at all had ever been there, but the former inhabitants were dead. In 1809, government officials tasked with mapping the coast arrived on the island and were greeted by the Indigenous locals. Things started off poorly, but the officials followed the unofficial directives and offered a gift of several thick blankets they'd kept separate in the hull of the ship—those on the ship had been vaccinated, and one of the men had survived a terrible case of smallpox himself. The true intent of the blankets worked well enough that six months after the governmental vessel departed Picture Island, the five remaining survivors departed themselves, in desperation, and were lost to history.

The fishermen and their families had chosen to build their homes in a clearing just off the eastern shore. They accidentally dug up a burial ground and had to move the bodies, and in doing so discovered that many of their party had not been vaccinated against smallpox—land scurvy they'd called it.

By 1819, Ghost Clearing had a store, a trading post, a saloon, a small lumber mill, and a church. Thirty-one habitations were scattered in close proximity to the docks. By 1929, the town had devolved: church, speakeasy, and trading post. In 2021, the town of Ghost Clearing had blossomed: five trinket stores (open during tourist season only), one grocery store, one hardware store, a restaurant (Frying High, again, seasonal), a Catholic Church, a school, more than three hundred cottages (most of the rental variety, and very small in stature), the fishery, the ten-man lumber mill, a government subsidized marina, a hotel with bar and eatery (Picture House Lodge), and a handful of other odds and ends establishments set up in sheds or the sunrooms at the front of homes.

James South pushed back from his seat at the far north corner of Picture House Lodge's large dining area, leaving behind a greasy plate and an empty coffee mug. The space was rustic: bare timber frame, worn green carpet, animal busts, old license plates from all over. Nearby, a young man sat at a table with a laptop and a cup of tea, otherwise the dining room was vacant. For now.

The supper crowd would move on in shortly, along with anyone arriving on the ferry—not that many would, especially not this weekend where on the mainland the Ghost Clearing Bears were favorites in a men's league slo-pitch tournament, taking with them approximately seventy percent of the town's locals as a booster club. The bigger draws on Picture Island, which was during the official tourist season, had yet to begin—the biggest of any time were the two weeks of the blackberry festival, which was still more than a month away—but visitors were fairly steady from the end of May onward.

James reached the till and rang the silver bell. "Coming!" Mandy Ng called out from someplace hidden. A door swung open, bringing a great waft of warm scents from a candle. "How many times you been here and can't figure out the price?"

James pulled a face: shock, offense. "If I left the money on the table, I wouldn't see your pretty face. Or your nice rump."

Mandy snorted. "Pancake booty. Nine-fifty."

James pulled out his wallet and then debit card, slowly. "I think your butt is cute."

Mandy raised an eyebrow. "And what good would that do me?"

James shrugged. "I like compliments, they make me feel good. Maybe compliments make you feel good."

The machine beeped between them and James sheathed his card and then deposited his wallet in the front left pocket of his Levi's.

"I like honesty," Mandy said and then tore free the freshly printed receipt.

"I am being honest."

Mandy had lost patience for this particular conversation, but acquiesced and said, "I like how the black in your beard streaks like lightning bolts through all the grey. It reminds me of the Bride of Frankenstein."

James ran a hand over his foot-long beard. "I see that too. Thank you." He nodded, almost curtsied. "You've made my day that much brighter. Face, booty, compliment, it's all coming up Milhouse."

Mandy rolled her eyes but was not displeased with James. He was a regular, he was nice, and a little bit interesting.

James started away, saying over his shoulder, "If you get any cuter, I'll have to dump Garth and switch teams."

"Go row your boat!" Mandy said.

Boating was indeed on James' to-do list for the evening, though unless he got very unlucky, there'd be no rowing involved. He had five crab traps, the furthest being twenty-five miles offshore along a rocky reef that extended almost all the way to the island like a speed bump for boats, and they needed regular monitoring. It seemed like unnecessary cruelty to leave an animal in a cage longer than required, especially when it was used to the whole damned Pacific.

His boat, a twenty-foot Thunder Jet, was docked almost exactly two hundred yards from the main doors of Picture House Lodge. After the brief walk, he boarded, started the engine, and began unmooring. A yawn escaped him as he rubbed a hand on the bulge of his belly. The older he got, the poorer his system dealt with carbs. If he ate a big burger and fries, he had to get busy almost right away to stave off the sudden and powerful sleepiness that would inevitably arise. He yawned a second time as he steered between the lines of bobbing vessels. Once into relatively clear waters, he reached around the cabin wall and pulled open the door on his electric cooler. Blindly, he withdrew a can of Diet Coke. He needed that caffeine.

In explanation, checking traps sounded a bit dull, but he loved the breeze against his ears and the briny scent of open water as it tickled into his sinuses. The waves played the red evening sun like loose harp strings, and he couldn't imagine living anywhere else. It took him close to an hour, but he was coming onto the bobbing marker of his fifth and final trap—the yield on the first four would pay for his suppers for the week, so that was a pleasant surprise. He lowered the throttle to nil and reached with his hook pole. He caught the rope beneath the marker and began dragging the trap up. Within seconds he noticed a problem.

A few problems in fact.

The least of which was that there were no crabs inside the trap. Next on the list, going from letdown to outright troublesome, there was a mystery of what those white chunks were stuck to the cage—like bleached and spotted shale slivers. The worst of all was that the cage was destroyed; most of it flattened, flatter than any pancake Mandy Ng had ever judged herself against.

"What in the heck?" he said.

The traps weren't designed to counter a great deal of weight, but someone would've had to drop one heck of a rock to squish it this badly. He set it down on the floor and crouched. He picked at the white chunks caught in the wires. They were like extra-thick eggshell, even had pale yellow haloes like some lizard eggs featured. But that couldn't be. This was too, too big, and imagine an egg crushing a steel structure. Even a semi-flimsy one.

"Impossible."

With a huff, James reeled in the bobbing marker and set a course for home. He knew a couple guys he could show the trap to—the main one being his husband, Garth—maybe they'd have a clue, but he doubted it. He could imagine the dumb questions: did a sea lion pull this up and smash it; did he put it somewhere a boat might've hit it; did he do something, anything; how was this *his* fault? It was enough to make him consider dumping the trap over the side without the marker on it, let it drift out of his life, eventually become a piece of the scenery. Someplace a small fish might one day evade the dinner plate of something bigger, at least temporarily.

He shook his head. He'd lived on the water a long time and he'd never seen anything quite like it. That alone was enough to take it in and see what was what.

4

Terror reigned until hunger conquered all else within the beast's mind. Instinct came on hunger's heels and the giant beast—a creature resembling an oversized ancestor of the modern alligator—rose from the cool and murky depths, chasing the evening sun and the chunky blob shadowing the in-between. Once close, the gator spread its jaws, ready to kill its first meal.

The chunky blob sensed it and rolled sideways. It had a face and eyes. It gave a second's glance at the gator and then darted away, cutting the familiar water like a bullet through belly fat. The gator watched the trail of bubbles rise and disappear and then followed them up. Once above the surf, it took its first self-sufficient inhalation—it had been working with the remainder of one-hundred-billion-year-old oxygen from within the egg, which had been stored in its lungs until then. In two directions, nothing but water. In the third, distant though it was, was green land. The fourth direction gave the beast pause and it ducked deep enough that only its eyes and nostrils remained above water. Huge, white, and loud, a ship carved great ripples as it headed toward Picture Island. The rumbling sound was incredible, terrible.

The gator dropped back beneath the surf and

waited out this menace. From below, it spotted the huge school of fish riding in the ship's drag. It appeared that this giant white vessel was a food giver, almost like a mother might be. The beast darted toward the small-minded fish and ate more than twenty at its first pass. This felt good, better than simply satiating hunger. This was its nature.

5

A shiny, black Ford Focus rode the ferry over behind Carole's BMW sedan and had, since docking and departing the ship, trailed her all the way into the Picture House Lodge parking lot. Carole's mother had a cabin, sure, but it was a little too rustic for Carole's tastes and a little too cozy, so whenever she and Shane had visited, they'd gotten a room to use as a home base.

"We ready?" she said, turning in her seat.

Alexis was on the verge of nodding off—sugar crash—and George simply bobbed his head once as he looked at his phone, the comics repacked away with the rest of his stuff.

"All right then," Carole said and swung open her door.

Two slots down in the mostly vacant lot, the Focus had parked and a skinny man stood by a rear door, pulling two large pieces of luggage free. He turned and hip-bumped the door closed. He hit the lock button on his fob, flashing the lights, and then started away across the paled and cracked asphalt of the lot, wheels playing that familiar tune as they went.

Carole got back to her business and stepped to the open and gently bobbing trunk lid. The wind was so much worse on the island than on the mainland—triple that when a storm hit—though it wasn't too bad this evening. Inside were her suitcase, which was a big black Samsonite on wheels, Alexis' pink The North Face backpack, and George's blue Nike duffle bag. Carole handed off the luggage accordingly before hefting out her bag and telescoping the handle so she could pull it comfortably.

"It smells funny," Alexis said as they crossed the parking lot, her trailing a smidge behind.

Carole looked back and kept walking, was about to overtake the man who'd gotten out of the Focus where he stood ten yards from the entrance. "Yeah, I don't—" The man put out his arm to stop Carole and George. "Excuse—"

"Bear," the man said and nodded to a grizzly bear yanking items from the dumpster—the cause of the smell. It was a big bear, but not massive by grizzly standards.

"Oh," Carole said and then whispered to the kids, "Wide berth." She led them on an ovular route to the door, giving the bear, which was never really between them and the door, plenty of space to forage for unwanted delicacies. Enough space that it would never feel threatened by their presence. Once inside, she said, "Have all your parts?"

"Bears don't eat people," Alexis said.

"Maybe, but they've been known to maul people. Way more dangerous than sharks," Carole said. Once she reached the desk, she hit the bell.

"Coming!" a disembodied voice shouted from somewhere beyond view. Mandy popped her head around a corner. "Oh, Carole! How's it going?"

Carole nodded over a shoulder. "You have a bear in your dumpster."

"Grizzly bear," George added solemnly.

Mandy's face scrunched tight and her eyes hardened. "Ooh that son of a…give me a sec," she said and retreated behind the wall. She reemerged seconds later with a rifle nearly as tall as she was. "Be right back."

Carole let go of her luggage handle and followed Mandy to the door, the kids tight behind her. Mandy stepped outside and got to about twenty feet from the bear. She then fired into the sky and began shouting, "Git! Git!" The bear fell off the lip of the dumpster and then scrambled to its feet before breaking for the thick forest surrounding just about everything on the island.

Carole held the door open when Mandy returned. She theatrically blew at the smoky barrel, showing off for the kids. At the desk, Carole said, "How did bears even get here?"

"First, someone brought deer so they could eventually hunt them for food. But the deer population boomed and they started getting in the way and eating more than just the grass. So they brought in four bears; lot more than four bears now, I tell you," Mandy said as she crossed behind the desk and once again out of view to stow the rifle.

"Grizzly bears eat deer?" Carole said, visibly surprised.

"Oh, yeah. It's awful too. Not very quick at all. Now, any specific room you'd like? Place is a ghost town this weekend." Mandy was back and had her hand on the computer mouse, awakening the system.

"No specific room. Mom told me about the baseball tournament."

Mandy handed over the keycards and her expression softened. "Very sad to hear about Shane."

Carole puckered her mouth and nodded. "Yes."

The man from the Focus came in then halfway grinning. "That bear's back."

"Son of a…gun!" Mandy said and stomped back around the wall to her office, returning once again with the long rifle in her smallish hands. "I'll be just one more minute."

6

Josephine Kincaid, Josie, stretched her dirty fingers, working out the achy kinks of arthritis. She then brushed her hands on the denim seat of her overalls shorts and leaned in once more to inhale the sweet aroma of the four-foot marijuana plants growing on her deck. It was so nice not to have to hide it anymore, though she wasn't quite sure what her daughter would say. Not that it mattered much; she was sixty-eight and for more than a decade, puffing marijuana had eased the pain in her joints better than anything her pharma-loving doctor on the mainland had ever prescribed. Nothing her somewhat uptight daughter could say was going to outweigh the factual results. Hell, maybe what happened with Shane was enough to jar loose some of the ties that had her so firm in her ways.

She pushed to her feet and stepped slowly, clumsily, to the barbeque. Even if they didn't sleep over every night on the island—and Josie didn't blame them, her home was small and a bit rough by modern standards—they did eat most meals there. She opened the valve on the propane tank and then clicked the igniter to life.

As if hearing a dinner bell, her cellphone buzzed in the front pocket of her Dickies. She awoke the ancient Kyocera and read, *Be there in half an hour.*

Kids hungry. Always.

"Don't I know it? Didn't I just turn on the barbeque?" she said, speaking to the fluffy white cat running its blocky head against the screen door that led into the home. "Back it up, Bozo." Josie kicked gently, nudging the cat deeper inside. She didn't let it stray far, there were too many predators out there and a chunky housecat was easy prey.

Josie shivered. It was cool up there. The temperatures on Picture Island were always moderate, even way up the hill where Josie lived; in the deep of winter it only tickled the freezing point. That meant outside late June through to early September, she had to wear at least a sweater even when she liked to let her legs breathe. Now, she buttoned the flannel she already had on and swung open the pantry closet door to retrieve her grilling apron—it featured a bikini babe bod and two pockets. She stashed her personal mixture of seasonings that she transported in old Club House containers. From the fridge she pulled the ground beef she had pre-rolled, the cheese slices—she'd settled for cheese slices years ago when her rare trips to the mainland left her with two choices: pay exorbitant prices for blocks when hers inevitably went too moldy for use or learn to enjoy the ageless stuff in the plastic wrap—and the aluminum tray of onions and banana peppers she had soaking up A-1 sauce. She set all that on the counter and returned to the fridge for the head of lettuce she'd picked a few hours earlier. Though her home was small, she had all the land she needed for a greenhouse, an outdoor garden—

which she begrudgingly shared with the local wildlife—a spot for a big campfire pit, and all the trees she could count.

"Out of the way," she said when Bozo came in looking for pets while she bent to retrieve a cutting board. Due to a lack of space, behind the cutting boards and pots and pans, were two-thirds of her personal armory: a .306 rifle and a .22 handgun. Leaned inside her jacket closet was a .22 rifle loaded with birdshot—this was mostly used to put a scare on animals; she didn't want to hurt anything, not really. Animals had no way of knowing they were upsetting her work by stealing, they were just hungry.

Her phone vibrated again and she set down the knife before making the first cut into the lettuce. She read, *Do you need me to grab anything?* She wiped a hand down the front of the apron and used two hands to type, *Only if you want a drink drink, only have a bottle of whiskey from who knows when.* She knew, of course. Shane brought it last time they'd visited nearly three years prior. Poor Shane.

She finished with the lettuce and then got out her homemade buns. She brought one up to her nose after cutting it and inhaled the sweet aroma. Lovely. After setting the table and lining the fixins along the counter, she returned to the porch and the barbeque. Her guests would arrive any minute and nobody liked to wait on supper.

7

Denver Jones had watched the grizzly inspect the dumpster pretty thoroughly by the time he went into the hotel to fetch the little woman with the long rifle. He wasn't used to the rural existence and considered what he'd seen nothing short of a hoot, considered the price of the room he rented a steal, and considered the décor within his room quaint. The TV was a massive RCA with a bulging back where it hid the tube and other dated guts while the screen rounded out in a way that reminded him of Saturday morning cartoons.

"Fantastic," he said and bounced his palm against the springy bed. In the corner was an old touch lamp in shades of faded copper. The nightstand didn't match the dresser, and neither matched the TV stand. The curtains were heavy and off-white. "Probably used to be a smoking room."

Denver had taken the week off and flown up to chase after the meteorite that had landed somewhere near Picture Island two days earlier. He'd been waiting for something like this, pushing ahead his vacation time until he sprung this news on his bosses. They were a little annoyed, a little amused. None of the current projects were coming down to the wire and all could understand to one degree or another, but the ocean was huge, the chances of his locating the element—that might just be anywhere or even nowhere—was like a pipedream. But what the hell?

Being an astronomer gave Denver a little more room for empathy from his coworkers. They'd all *love* to find a piece of space debris, especially one that entered the solar system as hot as this one had. They all likely had a history not so different from his, which meant they could see the potential where he did. When he was a kid, Denver dreamed of going to space. He dreamed of coaxing a friendly alien out of the forest with some Reese's Pieces. When he got older and the real world began falling into place and pointing out his personal limitations, he dreamed of developing a machine to roam other planets. He dreamed of seeing a version of himself played out on the big screen after achieving some great beyond feat. When he got into the shallow waters of an adulthood based on realism, he dreamed of being integral to something boundary pushing. He dreamed of discovering a planet or element, perhaps naming it. He dreamed of being first to do *something* special. Like, just maybe, be the one to locate a unique to Earth specimen that had barreled through the atmosphere and landed in the Pacific Northwest, not far from a barely inhabited island.

Though it wasn't exactly scientific, he planned to start at the bar. Asking the locals was bound to offer some false positives, but it took only one true positive to put him on-track. Attempting to fit in, he pulled on a green flannel jacket and slipped out

"Yeah, thank you," Denver said and accepted the eight-inch strip of translucent plastic. "So, uh, say, I'm in town trying to track down a meteorite; no chance any of you saw it fall two nights ago?"

One of the men said, "Wife did, said it was real close, but out in the water."

Mandy was at the tap behind the bar refilling Denver's glass. "Whereabouts, did she say, Henry?"

The man said, "Southwest."

Mandy nodded. "Lucy was in to check the schedule, said she'd been at the harbor, and James showed her one of his crab traps. He said it had been down below nine feet off that sandy ledge not far from Lion Island; something had come along and flattened it."

Lion Island was a smoothed rock that jutted like a water-damaged pyramid from the ocean. It was about twelve yards across and only sea lions, seagulls, and tourists paid it any mind. And the occasional hungry and ambitious orca whale.

"Must've been pretty heavy to cut the water?" one man said.

"Probably a boat," another said.

"There?" yet another said.

Mandy continued, "And he uses those heavy old cages."

"Flattened it, huh?" the insurance man said.

Mandy nodded and handed Denver his fresh beer and he waved his debit card.

"Where do I find James…?" Denver said.

"He's pretty early to bed most days, but he comes in for breakfast. I can leave a note that you want to speak with him. Fine if I give him your room number?" Mandy said.

"Absolutely." Denver could hardly believe this plausible lead came so quick and easy. He relaxed some, ready to talk about whatever these locals wanted to or simply sit and listen; having the information he did freed up some time and washed away most of the nervousness he felt around strangers.

The others started asking Denver questions and they all seemed fascinated that he'd done contracts for NASA. By his third beer, he was exaggerating, but the others were drinking it up, enjoying it—no harm, no foul. It was nice to be at the center of things.

8

A new problem crept slowly into the giant gator's world. Though the fish had been fresh and silky, the water wasn't quenching its thirst. The oddity of it set a low-scale panic into place and the gator surged up from the depths and breached the surface as if it might drink from the air. Overhead, the stars stretched out endlessly while a halfmoon shined blue light over the distant beach.

The beach was different and different was needed, so the gator headed in that direction, swaying in a rhythmic writhe that sent waves big enough to have come from a Jet-ski; though unlike the personal pleasure cruiser, the gator moved in silence. The shore came up quickly and the gator took its first clumsy steps on land. A few feet away, a squirrel stood on its hindlegs, considered the massive beast, and then bolted up the rocky ascension into the woods.

The gator paused, stiffening its stance, forcing its knees to quit shaking. Once the gator trusted itself to walk, it began trailing another water sound. This time no thoughts needed arise, instinct pushed it toward the source.

A rusty steel culvert jutted from the rocky wall of the shore and water rushed down toward the ocean. The gator put its great jaws around the culvert like a straw and let the icy-cold water spill onto its tongue. Freshwater. It drank to full and then some, and only stopped drinking when it heard another new sound and strange new lights flashing down the beach, approaching. The gator slipped back into the ocean and swam until only its eyes and nostrils remained topside. It watched as two strange figures walked by, waving flashlights and conversing, unaware that they were twenty feet away from the largest predator Picture Island had ever seen.

9

"How you holding up?" Josie said to her daughter. She'd put the mesh bug screen down around her deck and the pair sat out there with glasses of sweet tea. Josie also had a pinner joint she was—quite literally—aching to burn.

"I'm a little surprised how good I've been… Shane and me, we drifted apart, mostly it was the kids thing. I don't know why he…that's not true, I never cared to know why or come to understand how deeply against the idea he was. I wanted them and now I have them," Carole said.

"But you don't have him…seems extreme," Josie said, the final bit coming through a cloudy exhalation. She held out the joint. "Want a hit?"

Carole waved it away. "I've never liked it. I always think I'm peeing."

"Maybe try edibles," Josie said.

"I remember one time we were watching that movie, *'Salem's Lot*. I got mad at the battered woman for not leaving her stupid trucker husband after she was riding along with a black eye and then Shane turned to me and said, 'Where could she go?' Then I got mad at him and he says, 'Imagine our roles are reversed. I've been following you around while you take on better and better jobs while the gaps in my resume keep on getting wider. The last ten places I applied to didn't even call me.' I didn't even know he'd been trying to supplement the little income he made with those silly books."

"That's no reason to kill yourself."

"Yeah, well, maybe it was the simplest thing. I don't know. He could've left…I knew he was unhappy about the kids, but he'd been unhappy about moving so much and got over that, too."

Josie exhaled. "Did he?"

"I don't know. I guess he must've. I never really thought about it. I was furthering my career. For us."

"What about his career?"

"Writing?" Carole scrunched up her face. "He never said anything…I mean, sometimes he hinted that it would be cool to check out places or sign up for an expensive course… Doesn't matter now, does it?"

"Guess not. How did the kids take it?"

"Alexis cried but got over it the quickest. She didn't know him that well. George has been pretty quiet since, and he reads all Shane's old books and comics. He seems okay."

Josie stubbed out the little roach in a tea saucer she'd used as an ashtray for many years now. "He didn't see Shane hanging there, did he?"

"No! No way… I don't think—no! Couldn't have," Carole said, and she'd clearly never considered it a possibility.

"I certainly hope not," Josie said and then stood. "I'm guessing you're heading back to the hotel?"

"Yeah. Too cramped and too…outdoorsy."

Josie gave a giggle. Her eyes were glossy and a slight grin had begun to rise. The first twenty minutes after burning were her favorite—when she could let herself be high.

It took a few minutes, but Carole had the kids awakened from either ends of her mother's couch and into the car. Alexis sat up front, expression cloudy with exhaustion. George sat in the back, somberly looking at the darkness beyond his window. Driving was slow over the meandering forest road and for the entire twenty-nine-minute trek, Carole thought about George maybe seeing Shane, but she couldn't bring herself to ask. Especially not with Alexis in the car, even dopey as she was.

In the hotel lobby, they passed the man who'd driven behind them off the boat. He was visibly tipsy and quite possibly hitting on the owner of the Picture House Lodge, Mandy Ng. Carole realized then that she'd never thought to ask anything about the woman. Now, thanks to Josie pointing it out, she wondered how egocentric she was in the other parts of her life. Was she this way at work? Was she this way with friends?

As she brushed her teeth, she came to the conclusion that she could safely blame Shane alone for what he'd done for two reasons: one, suicide was an easy way to make any survivor feel guilty, and two, he was too dead to defend himself so she could see it any way that it fit how she wanted to see it. She rinsed her mouth and hit the light. Through the heavy darkness of the room, she found the vacant option of the two queen beds. Within minutes, she'd cast aside any troublesome internal dialogue and snored gently with her cheek against the pillow.

10

As Denver Jones rarely drank alcohol, especially not to excess, he was never quite ready for the hangover that inevitably struck the following mornings. Like this morning. He pushed from the bed, the phone in his room ringing at a volume to wake the dead. He crawled across the stiff rug and picked up the hard white receiver.

"Hello?" he said and then burped. "Sorry, hello."

"I think I have the wrong room," a husky voice said.

"Okay." Denver unthinkingly cradled the receiver and leaned back against the dresser. He drank in the room and awoke a little further. He *was* waiting for a call. "Oh, you b—" The phone rang again and he lashed out a hand. "Hello?" he said, stern and ready.

"I did have the right room."

"Yes, you woke me up. I apologize."

"No worries. Mandy left a note for me with my breakfast order that you wanted to chat?" James South said.

"You have a crushed crab trap?"

"That's right and it was covered in big chunks of thin white stone."

"Stone?"

"Think so. Look, my breakfast's getting cold. I'll be down here until nine. If you want to go take a look at the trap, we can. I even kept all that stone—stuff, I guess."

"Yes, right. Absolutely," Denver said. "Be down soon. Don't leave early."

"I won't."

Denver pushed to his feet and nearly fell with the rush of blood and the striking spike that lodged itself in the front of his brain. He stumbled to his bag and found the travel kit where he kept all the just in case items one might need while hunting down a bit of space debris. He popped the top on the Tylenol bottle and slipped three coated capsules onto his tongue. He then pushed on into the washroom and began drinking water by the handfuls from the tap. The coldness was heaven.

Fourteen minutes later, Denver was shaved, showered, and smelling fresh. He'd dressed in another set of clothes that he thought would fit the calling, and they nearly matched what he'd worn the night before—though this time there were no lingering stickers. He crossed the lobby and waited by the entrance to the bar and dining area. The smell of beer permeated the atmosphere and he had to swallow four consecutive, convulsive gags before he had control of himself. Two big men with beards approached him and he forced himself straight.

"You Denver, the scientist?"

Denver nodded and held out a hand. "Yes, thank you for meeting me."

James South shook and when he let go, Denver

reached for the other man's hand.

"I'm James and this is my husband Garth," James said.

Garth let go of Denver's hand and then turned to James. "Off to the grind. Meet for supper?"

James nodded and Garth carried on his way. "He works for the National Park. Whole north end of the island is National Park. We have more varieties of snakes, frogs, and spiders than anywhere else in the Pacific Northwest."

"I did not know that," Denver said and stepped in tune when James started toward the exit.

"The trap's in my shed at home. Not even a quarter mile, so we can walk...but I guess you might want to collect something from the...stone, or whatever?"

"Probably that would be easiest. So, take my rental car?" Denver said.

James didn't complain an iota when he had to stuff himself into the Ford Focus and Denver said nothing in apology, though he wanted to. Decided best to leave it unacknowledged. They rolled twice as far as the walking distance; the conversation kept strictly to directions. Denver pulled in next to Garth's departing work truck—bright yellow with an orange flasher mounted to the roof and a wench above the front bumper. Garth waved and both Denver and James waved. As if making up for the—hopefully—good fortune of locating James and the ruined trap, the day was turning into a poorly executed joke.

Getting out of the car was even more difficult than getting in for James. The Ford rocked on its springs and Denver had the slightly drunk image of himself and the big fisherman riding those coin operated vehicles outside grocery stores and department stores. He looking silly and the bigger man absolutely dwarfing the machine that moved despite the weight on it while carnival music played in the background.

"This way," James said, waving over his shoulder and ripping Denver from reverie.

"Yep," Denver said and followed the man into a rough cedar building just about big enough to park a Cadillac Escalade inside, or maybe a boat. The middle, most of the floor in fact, was empty and fluorescent lighting ran in two rows along the ceiling. There were two work benches, one either of the long sides. On the one to the left was the squished trap.

"So, what do you think?"

Denver stepped in close next to the trap and picked up the stone that, upon close inspection, was not stone at all. "This isn't rock. This filmy underlayer, it's more like…" he trailed.

James saw it then. "Egg?"

"Biggest egg I've ever seen. Any ocean…?" he trailed again. The only thing that might've made something that big was a whale, but whales were mammals and did not lay eggs.

"I don't have any clue. Oh! What if it's whale sperm coating something…no, it'd stink, and it comes in huge wads."

Denver almost said *Comes in huge wads, huh?* but bit it down. It was a drunken thought, a joke he might've made last night while flying high in the company of men awed by him. "You don't mind if I take some of this, correct?"

"That's why we drove, isn't it?"

Denver nodded and selected two large chunks and took them to the trunk of the rental. Once he got back to the mainland where there were department stores and whatnot, he'd pack it up and figure out somewhere to send it. He swung closed the trunk and said, "Will you show me where? I can cover gas or whatever."

James waved this off. "No need, but I'll take you. We'll walk to my boat, it's not far. Don't think my knees can take another ride in that clown car."

Denver nodded. Probably shouldn't be driving anyway, he decided; he was obviously still a little beer woozy.

11

Carole waved Josie down when she saw her enter the hotel lobby. She had on a big floppy sunhat, shorts, and a hoodie. Strapped sandals on her feet. She also had a bulky backpack slung over her shoulder.

"Thought maybe the kids would like to do some treasure hunting," she said, calling it out, still fifteen feet away. She half turned to show off the bag. The head of a metal detector wand jutted out the top.

George looked up from a reprint issue of *Weird Science*. He nodded once. "Cool," he said and it was the first thing he'd said all morning, aside from ordering pancakes with bacon and a glass of orange juice from a waiter.

Josie quit walking and waited for her family to reach her before turning and leading the way. Without discussion, they went to a gold and brown Jeep Cherokee from the mid-eighties. Josie had left the back gate open a crack; she'd obviously wanted to tease the kids with her pack and hadn't actually needed to pull it out beforehand. She swung it wide and the sweet aroma of marijuana wafted out. She stashed the bag while the kids climbed in the back seat.

Carole snatched Josie by the wrist and hissed, "You're not high, right?"

Josie yanked her hand away. "I'm almost never high, just a little numb, thank goodness for that too. If it were up to the docs, I'd be another sore junkie, popping more and more pills until I became a zombie."

"Yeah, well, the kids…you know…and driving."

Josie rolled her eyes. "Who's whose mother here?"

"Whatever," Carole said and stepped around to the shotgun seat.

The Jeep rumbled to life and they headed along the skinny coastal road until turning onto a path that quickly became dirt and widened out into a parking lot. There was a small patch of sand and miles of rocky shore. The tide was out some and that would give them a little more space to treasure hunt.

"Where'd you get that thing anyway?" Carole said as Josie pulled the two halves of the metal detector's shaft from her pack.

Josie leaned it sideways for a look, as if it might have a sales sticker to jog her memory. "Amazon. Where else?"

"Oh."

"I have Prime. Not near as fast as they promise but anyone living on Picture Island is wise to leave impatience at the door." Josie had the machine together and held out the bulky headphones. "The eldest child has to go first when it comes to listening for metal."

"No, me," Alexis said, arms folded, huge pout on her mug.

"Sorry, girlie, rules are rules," Josie said and then got into explaining how the metal detector worked.

Carole zoned out, watching a boat a good ways offshore, bobbing next to what appeared to be a massive boulder, one that jutted hugely above the surf. The constant echo of sea lion barks played background soundtrack to the affair while their dark blobby shapes moved around the rock. Beyond all that, the ferry was making one of its morning crossings. It began the journey over to Picture Island at 7:05 AM, left at 9:20 AM, began another return trip at 4:00 PM, and finally finished the day with a trip to the mainland leaving Picture Island at 6:25 PM. It was all very tedious to the locals, but riding was fun when it wasn't absolutely necessary—during visits and the likes. Particularly for children.

"You coming?" Josie called from the beach.

Carole offered a subdued grin and began walking. What her mother had said last night came back, frothy waves lapping at the shore of her mind. Had George seen Shane? And then, after that, almost as uncomfortable, was she really that self-centered?

Josie and the kids hooted and booed—mostly Josie and Alexis, but Josie was working a bit of magic on George, too—as they scanned the sopping rocks and the wads of seaweed. Carole stretched on a blanket and withdrew her phone. She'd downloaded an eReader app and was finally, finally going to read one of Shane's books, horror or no. So far in the story, she'd only gotten to a husband and wife and the resemblance to her existence undressed her mentally. She hadn't known he'd written so thinly veiled renditions of them, not that she ever asked and she guessed maybe that she never did ask gave him the freedom to express things. She talked to people about her problems and he wrote down his problems. She had never considered that when he didn't want to talk to her about things it was because he was built differently and instead put it all down on paper.

"I am selfish," she said and then flipped out of the eReader app to try her luck with Instagram. There was cell service on the island, but it was slow, so she had to wait every three posts and two crashed video ads. She set her phone aside, frustrated, and watched the ferry. Within seconds a great grinding sound rang out and two heads on the small boat popped up like perfect shadowy spheres. The ferry slowed some but continued on its passage. The heads on the smaller boat bent back out of view.

An idea hit. Carole glanced down the beach. Now Alexis had the huge headphones on, metal detector riding her arm, while George carted the little shovel. Carole lifted her phone and opened the camera app. She zoomed as far out as it would go and tried to hold the two, very pixelated men in the frame. One was the man from last night, the one who'd followed them off the boat. A fresh and unusual thought came then and she wondered if he was single. She gasped. Not once since Shane had done what he'd done had her subconscious presented that particular question.

12

The world was loud and bright. The giant gator scurried out to the deeper ocean with the passing of the first automobile on the road above. After that came the giant white vessel that sent an incredible rumble through the water. The gator dove deep to get away and watch for schools of fish, but it didn't really work. That rumble was awful. No longer giving, this ship seemed threatening.

Once it ceased, the gator forgot about it and hunted fish and two smallish sea lions. It tried for a duck, but the duck was too slick and too small to be worth fussing over. Then came the other cutting noise, a buzz rather than a rumble. The gator watched and then followed, curious. It was irritating, but not jarring. It stopped not far from something like a meal platter—that big rock loaded with barking creatures that glistened wetly beneath the sun. Without really deciding on anything, there was no doubt that the gator would visit that rock and those sea lions, but only once it was safe to do so.

It crept close to the boat once it stalled and watched the upright figures as they leaned over the side of the boat. These were the same as the ones on the beach from the night before, or not quite the same. Same species, certainly.

The incredible rumble came close again and the gator had to swim far, far out to get off the shelf and fall into the very deep waters. It watched as the giant thing approached…approached its home, intruded on its space. Minutes passed and, though the gator was much smaller than the huge white shape that threatened the world with its rumbling song, it darted at full speed, spinning at the last second to lash out with its armored tail. The bang was great and black fluid spilled into the waters. Half the rumble instantly silenced, but the vessel hadn't changed course at all, only speed.

This ship was too formidable. Rethinking this assault, the gator hurried back to the dark depths as one of the ferry's propellors had ceased spinning and now only spilled black fluid.

13

Mandy rolled from bed and to the can. It had been a strange night, and a long night. Typically, she slept and remained on-call when things were that dull. During the busier times, she had overnight employees.

That scientist had chatted her up, drunk as he was, and it was more than a little bit interesting. A meteorite—which turned out to be a chunk of an asteroid that had made it through Earth's atmosphere, thus taking on the separate terminology—had fallen somewhere nearby, and he was going to find it. She asked if it was worth anything and it took him a minute to understand that she was asking if finding it was like hitting your numbers on the lotto. Almost certainly not, but precious minerals on Earth were found on other planets, so it was possible the meteor was one giant diamond. Though wildly unlikely.

He'd then tried to parlay that into some joke about diamonds and girls and had anyone given her a diamond while he grinned with horny drunk menace. She'd told him no, which wasn't entirely true to what he was asking. No, she'd never received a diamond, but only because her ex-husband had proposed with a cubic zirconia on a band that quickly turned her finger Shrek green. Those felt like the before times and she sometimes thought longingly of a man in her bed, snuggled up beside her, but usually only in an abstract way. She didn't need all the body odor and dirty laundry and messy toilets—she had enough of that with the hotel. And most of that felt behind her, though hardly any of the white clientele—and four of five to visit Picture Island were white—could seem to tell that she was only three years from sixty. Not that that was something to complain about. Being appreciated physically, in the right kind of way, was a nice boost for her self-esteem. Even when she didn't think she needed it.

Showered and dressed, she took the back corridor that connected her room to the service hallway. She entered the kitchen and grabbed a mug from the pile not yet set out for the wait staff to place on tables. She stepped only far enough into the dining area to grab a coffeepot and filled her mug while she held open the swinging door with her hip. It was important to stay out of sight when she wasn't working yet.

Back in the kitchen, she had the cook whip up a grilled cheese. She sat flicking around the internet with a tablet, sitting at a table out near the walk-in cooler. A table typically reserved for the cook and the dishwasher for use during their breaks. She'd only just brushed the greasy crumbs from her fingers when an alert popped up and she read that the ferry from the mainland was laboring on its way home, and that early thoughts suggested a rotor must've tangled in fishing nets and blown.

"…I'm on the vessel and I heard the bang, it was incredible…"

Mandy looked at the byline. Stacy Brune was the local reporter who sold stories to any paper or magazine or website willing to take them. And there were enough of them all told that he eked out a living; though if done deftly, almost any living could be eked out on Picture Island without a great deal of income.

"Likely he was headed over to shoot some baseball pics," she said into her mug before she drained it. She wondered then if there'd be delays in the ferry schedule over the busted rotor—if it was exactly what they expected—and just how many mostly down days she might get to enjoy.

If the brunt of the town was off watching baseball and nobody new was coming in, there were likely only thirty or forty humans total on the island. That might give her sufficient time to tag along with the scientist, if he was still interested in having her around when he was sober. She, for some unnamable reason, thought he might, though she'd have to be upfront: she was only in it for the science and not romance.

"Ought to live a little," she said as she rose to bus her dishes back to the kitchen. She wasn't officially working until that evening, but decided she'd mull around a bit, just in case Denver Jones appeared with another offer of scientific exploration.

Janice was on the concierge desk doing mostly nothing, which was fine with Mandy because Janice's husband drank sixteen bucks in beer profits nearly every night and now and then, Janice and her friends made a night of it at the hotel. When only one game in town offered booze, the house always won.

"You see that scientist guy leave yet?" Mandy said.

Janice looked up from Twitter and blinked. "The guy who James called? The note guy?"

"Yes."

"Yeah, they left pretty early."

This made Mandy smile. James probably had him up and out after only five or six hours of sleep and quite likely fostering a hangover. "Great, carry on." Mandy tapped the desk and headed for the lobby doors.

14

Slow didn't begin to express how the morning had gone. Stewart Russell had organized his filing cabinet, sorted paperwork—typically his assistant's job, but she was on the mainland watching her husband play baseball—and made a list of clients who would possibly go for a mix-up with their insurance, which would, in-turn, give him fresh new commissions. He'd finished all that time burn by ten-thirty.

Now at a quarter to twelve, spinning on his desk chair, Adele blasting from the little JBL speaker next to his computer, he decided to shut it down for lunch, possibly the entire day. He had two choices for dining; he didn't have to cook himself and went with the Subway takeout bar attached to the ferry terminal. Meatball on Italian with a side of Tums to keep the inevitable heartburn at bay.

"Hear any updates?" he asked the pimply young man working behind the sneeze guard. He couldn't be sure, but thought he'd dated this kid's mother back in high school. Things like that happened a lot on Picture Island, right until someone either settled with the familiar and possibly related or went to the mainland and caught some fresh meat.

"About the ferry?" the kid asked. "No real updates. Last I heard it was still puttering over."

Stewart whistled at that. Should've landed half an hour ago. "How slow are we talking?"

The kid pointed a long knife at the ticket booth. "Sherry said they were about halfway, and that was twenty minutes ago, or so."

Stewart whistled again. "Geez Louise." The kid punched up the total after slipping his gloves off and Stewart withdrew his debit card. "Debit."

"Hear there's a guy looking for a comet?" the kid said as the receipt printed.

"Met him last night. He's looking for a meteorite. It's different after it makes it to Earth. Apparently. He was very particular about that fact."

The kid snatched the receipt and waved it over his head, blowing a hiss out. "Comet, asteroid, meteorite, star, I don't know any of that stuff."

"Me either, but the scientist was explaining it well enough despite being in his cups. I pretty much know insurance…say, how old are you? You know you can get a cheap policy that would pay you eight hundred bucks if you ever needed stitches."

The kid laughed. "No thanks."

Stewart grinned. "Man's got to try."

The kid nodded and Stewart took his footlong, his cookies, and a tall cup of Diet Coke back to his Cadillac. He drove out to the only section of beach near town and parked next to Josie Kincaid's Jeep Cherokee. They'd set up in the sand—where he'd planned on going—so he pulled the canvas camping chair out of the trunk and plunked down right by the front bumper of his car. He watched the kids for a while, watched Josie and her daughter a little less. They were searching for something, probably anything, but maybe meteorite bits.

"Could be a fever," he said, imagining the entire town getting into the act, streaming to the beach in droves, combing through sand and silt and seaweed. Some lunk-head would stumble onto it and probably try to get an arm and a leg from the scientist for it.

Stewart let his gaze play out onto the water. James South's boat was buzzing toward harbor and it appeared he had a passenger. Stewart's guess was that was the scientist right there. He finished his sandwich and balled the waxy paper as he watched the distant black sea lions, pretty much blobs to the naked eye from that far. Though there was no mistaking them, not with all the barking they did. Things never shut up and…

"What in the heck is that?" Stewart mumbled around a bite of cookie. He blinked hard once to clear anything that might qualify as figment. He looked again, leaning forward on his chair. A massive shape, like some kind of dragon, had risen from the ocean and burst up onto the rock face of Lion Island. Its rear end swung violently as it moved with fantastic speed. It chomped one and then two sea lions while the others scattered and barked faster and louder. Panic barking.

"Hey, Stewart."

He turned, wide-eyed, and pointed his cookie hand out for Josie to look, too. He shifted his attention, caught just the tail of the beast sliding back into the ocean.

"What was that?' Josie said.

"What was what?" Carole said, coming up behind her mother.

"Like…some kind of…" Stewart nearly said dragon. "Some kind of lizard."

"Sure it wasn't an orca?" Josie said, squinting.

Stewart gave that a moment's thought and then began nodding some. "Yeah, that's probably right. The distance is playing tricks on my eyes. Getting old, I guess."

"You're not as old as me," Josie said.

"How come they're barking so much?" Alexis said. Her face was red and even in the moderate heat and slightly overcast sky, she'd gotten burnt.

"Having a party," Carole said.

George was still down at the beach but was looking at Lion Island. He then bolted up to the parking lot. He stopped next to his aunt and looked at her. "Was that an alligator?"

All faced the kid a moment. He was young, probably had the best eyes because of it, but an alligator…nah.

"Had to be an orca. Sometimes they jump up," Josie said.

"Had to be," Stewart said, though he didn't really believe it. He thought once he got back into town, he might have a chat with James, maybe see if Garth knew of anything evasive that had come around, and if he was still there, ask the scientist what he thought. All that extra education had to account for something practical.

15

James had stripped to his trunks and dove into the cold water to take shots for the scientist. Normally he wasn't this helpful, but the idea that a meteorite had landed on his crab trap was a whole hell of a lot interesting. Something he could tell folks about for years to come. He had to act quickly, with every foot deeper and every minute longer, the water seemed to decrease in temperature. He came up shivering, but his waterproof camera had twenty shots and thirty seconds of night vision video. Hopefully there was something.

On the way back to the island, James could tell Denver was a little down about finding very little additional traces of what had landed on the crab trap, both were thinking maybe the two happenings had nothing to do with one another. "Wonder what happened to the ferry," he said.

Denver shrugged. "You haven't heard of any other strange occurrences in the water in the last couple days, have you?"

"You mean like a meteorite?"

Denver shrugged again.

The poor guy. He'd gotten his hopes up and James supposed that was unwise business in the slow world of science—wasn't everything in space already like a thousand years dead?

By the time they'd reached land, Denver was ravenous and offered to buy James lunch at the hotel. "I'm having supper there and three meals in one restaurant, in a day, is a bit much. But thank you," James said.

"Can I call you if I have any questions? Oceanic expertise might answer something right away that I'd spend a week confused about," Denver said and then yawned.

"Sure thing," James said and waved like a statute when the Ford began backing out the lane.

Inside, he turned on the TV and set to making himself a can soup. It hadn't even reached lukewarm when a knock landed against his door. He withdrew his phone from his pocket to see if he'd missed a text warning that someone was coming, but no.

"Huh?" he said and started across the vast timber frame main floor that featured only four walls and a divider between the kitchen and living room. It was the weekend, there'd be no mail, so he could only guess that perhaps it was Denver and he'd forgotten something...but Denver had his number. He swung open the door. "Oh, Stewart. What can I do for you?"

Stewart took a deep breath and blew it out heavily. "I've been doing some math in my head after what I think I saw and then your crushed trap...can I have a glass of water?"

"Oh, yeah, sure. Come on in."

"Thanks."

"You okay?" James went to the cupboard for a

tall glass.

"I don't know. Problem is, the kid saw what I saw, so did Josie, but she thought it was an orca. But she's older than me and has pretty thick glasses."

James ran the water. It was so bubbly that it looked smokey until the high mineral content began to settle. All the island's water came from a natural reservoir and brought along a little of just about everything the island was made of. "Saw what?"

Stewart laughed nervously as he accepted the glass of water. "My first thought was a dragon."

James frowned. "A dragon, huh?"

"Yeah," Stewart said and sipped from the water glass. "But that kid. Carole McNaughton's up, and that kid, must be one of the ones she inherited." Everyone on the island knew the story, all the way around and down the middle. "He said it looked like a gator, and damned if it didn't, but huge. Like long enough that Josie thought it was an orca."

"Where was this?" James would have sent this man packing if he weren't so visibly shaken. No matter how it sounded, he'd seen something.

"Lion Island. I saw your boat, were you over there?"

James leaned on the granite countertop. "I was. Not fifty feet from the island was where my trap got smooshed. But how would a gator get into the ocean?"

"I don't know…it was huge, maybe a crocodile somehow swam from Australia?" Stewart said after draining his glass.

"Think those are all freshwater." James tapped his counter three times. "What's say you and me go out with the fish finder and locate the thing if we can." He hadn't thought of this with the meteorite because a meteorite wasn't doing much moving after it landed. "You can record it on your phone, likely be good for business. When was the last time an insurance salesman went viral for discovering an out of place fish?"

This steadied Stewart some, though he remained leery. "Not a fish… And that thing looked awfully big."

"Can't hurt us if we stay in the boat."

"No, but really, it looked big enough that it could."

James tilted his head. "You know, stuff like *Jaws* doesn't happen in real life."

"Sure, but…oh, all right," Stewart said.

"Perfect, we'll go after I down this bowl of soup."

16

It was a bit of a trek, but after returning to the hotel to grab the car and a bite, and then following Josie home, the group paraded along the dirt trail through the woods toward the hot springs. Most days when the weather was above freezing, they were an attraction to tourists and locals alike. Alexis wanted to bring the metal detector since they hadn't found any treasure on the beach, just rusty fishing junk and clips from duffel bags or tents or whatever. Josie said it would be just more heartbreak. Carole said they already had enough to carry with the cooler, the towels, and the bug spray. George said nothing. While they'd eaten, he had rushed upstairs and from his inherited stash of comic books, he found an issue of *Unexpected* with a huge metallic gator on the cover that he just had to re-read—and did so on the ride. They reached the hot springs—finally silencing the irritating jingle of the bear bell attached to Josie's pack— and discovered they had it to themselves. There was about a fifty-fifty chance someone else might've been there, even with the ball tournament. This was nice, privacy was a bonus.

Or, at least, privacy from humans.

Used to people, the deer stayed fairly close to the family, though not close enough to touch.

There had to be a dozen of them. Oftentimes people fed them while they cooked in the steamy water, it kept the animals observable.

"Can I pet one?" Alexis said. She wore a one-piece that had gotten too small, putting it on a list of things to replace within Carole's head.

"Not likely," Josie said. "Deer are skittish. It's okay, looking's almost as good as touching."

"No it's not," Alexis said, pouty.

"Okay, but deer are like people. You wouldn't want strangers walking up and touching you, would you?"

"Yes," Alexis said sullenly.

Josie rolled her eyes. "Maybe we can get one to trust you enough to feed after supper, okay? There's plenty around."

The conversation stopped there for a good while. Alexis relaxed herself and floated like a starfish between the others who rimmed the pool—which was about five times as big as a hot tub. The pools all had uneven floors, a couple dipping to twenty feet below ground level. They stayed until they were good and wrinkly. They got out and began drying off when the sound of several animals skittering into motion gave them pause. As if out of nowhere, a grizzly was suddenly right there before them on its fours. Nobody spoke and nobody moved. Those glassy black eyes registered each face and all the humans gawked in frozen quiet, until George screamed, "Rawr!" with his hands up like claws and startled the bear. It took a step back and then after a tick, prattled away down the path, not so much bothered as disinterested.

The others looked at George. He was red-faced and breathing heavy.

"Bell doesn't work when we're not walking," Josie said. "Be fine as long as we keep moving."

17

Mandy stopped by Denver's table. He had a meal's worth of empty plates before him, two glasses, and an empty coffee mug. "How's the search going?" she said.

"I think I've hit a dead end, like smack," he said, and then brought his palms together like fleshy cymbals.

Much of the pep had gone out of him and Mandy was reconsidering reminding him of his offer to let her accompany him. "Oh, that's no good," she said.

He sat up straight and pointed a finger at her. "Maybe you can give me a second opinion on something."

"Sure," she said.

Denver stood and looked at the table. "I'll pay and then we'll go out to my car."

"Your car?"

"Sure, I want to show you something," he said and stood.

"Show me what?" Mandy said, thinking she ought to get it out of the way right now that she wasn't interested in anything more than the science and the distraction that came along with it.

"I want to hear what you make of it before I put

any ideas into your head."

Mandy said, "Hmm," a little reluctant, but ultimately willing to play along. While he paid, she stepped to the exit—it was odd to wait for someone in her own establishment. She felt like she looked like a silly schoolgirl with a crush, but the voice of age and wisdom boomed: *Who cares? You aren't that, so who cares?* Once she saw him coming, she stepped outside and inhaled deeply of the warm afternoon air.

"I'm parked over here," he said and motioned a waved with his right arm, though his fingers remained closed around a set of keys. The lights of a black Ford flashed and the trunk opened, bobbing gently as if on a wave. "What does this look like to you?" he said once he reached the back of the car.

Mandy looked in at the large, rounded chunks of white…something. "Can I touch it? Is it meteorite?"

"You can touch it, but it certainly wouldn't survive a fall through the atmosphere. So, no, not meteorite."

Mandy reached in. One side was completely smooth, while the other side was roughened slightly, sort of pitted. In between was a plasticky film. "Eggshell. But that can't be?" This came out like a question because she didn't know everything, not even close, and was fully willing to learn something new.

"That's what I thought, too. But it's massive. If it's shaped like any other egg…look how gentle the curve is." He began miming out what he thought.

"Nothing has eggs that big," Mandy said. The

curve and his miming suggested something about large enough to engulf the Ford.

"Right. So, what's your second thought?"

Mandy reached in and touched it again. Let her fingertips play over the almost solid white outer surface. She then leaned in and sniffed it. It pretty much smelled like the ocean and a bit like rental car. "I don't have any second thoughts. It seems like a giant egg."

Denver rubbed his chin. "Only eggs ever that big were dinosaur eggs, but a dinosaur egg would've long since fossilized. And the next question is, what's it doing crushing crab traps?"

"Did you call someone?"

"No. What I'm thinking is there's something logical and silly and I just need to show this to the right local and…you know, poof." He flared open his hands and his eyes.

"If there are two right locals it's James and Garth. Garth has some big-time animal education; I don't remember what. I'm guessing James showed Garth first and that's the only reason they'd need to show you, since you have other education and you're looking for something in particular. Neither of those guys exaggerate or lose their heads."

"I suppose I can call someone…I'd planned to, but the more and more that time passes, the less I'm thinking this has anything to do with why I'm here. I'll ship them off once I get to the mainland," Denver said and reluctantly closed the trunk lid. "I just wish there was some logical clue."

"Could have it been inside an asteroid and then the asteroid was so hot that when it began passing through the atmosphere, which then it became a meteorite," she touched her right ear to show she'd been listening, "it exploded when it hit the water, thus freeing the egg?"

"I get what you're saying… Ice. If the center of the meteorite were a massive chunk of ice, semi-protected by thick enough rock, then maybe it crushed the trap before boiling off and leaving debris from… Holy cow! What if it is an egg? It was on an alien planet in a different solar system. The planet went kaboom and pieces of egg were frozen in the water. Alien race egg!" He faced her and had a sparkle in his eyes as he grabbed her by the shoulders.

"No," Mandy said, thinking she saw what was coming next.

Denver closed his eyes and said, "Woo-saw, woo-saw. Not likely, that would be number one best case scenario…but Mandy, you've brightened my day quite a bit." He squeezed her shoulders gently.

She imagined him leaning in for a kiss then and decided now was going to be most opportune to explain her romantic disinterest. "I'm only here because it's interesting."

"What?" He dropped his hands, only then seeming to notice he'd touched her at all.

"Uh," *how to word it,* "last night you were coming onto me, I think, and I think you're smart and nice, but I'm only interested in the science, or, I guess, in that the science is a change from the norm. My norm."

"Oh. Okay, yes, great…sorry if I was… Let's

hope, uh…the most plutonic space egg discovery ever," he said, obviously testing a joke and if it weren't for Mandy's pity laugh, it would've fallen flat.

18

At first, Stewart had been worried they'd find the gator but now he was worried they wouldn't find anything beyond run of the mill oceanic life. Not even so much as an interloper from a faraway area. Fish, seals, sea lions, one distant humpback, but nothing beyond that. The only thing that eased the agony for Stewart was that James really wanted to find something. An explanation to what had happened to his crab trap was the minimum. He was set on a special discovery.

They'd buzzed and stopped, buzzed and stopped, circling Lion Island, going further and further out. Now they sat, gently swaying on the surf, both baked. Stewart had stripped down to his undershirt but was thinking he'd soon have to put it back on. According to his phone, they'd been out there for four hours.

"Well," he said.

James sat in the captain's chair, only slightly interested in the sonar readout. "Yeah, looks like a bust. Whatever it was must've taken off."

"Guess so."

"Let's say we take it slow back to shore, maybe we get lucky."

"Sure, whatever," Stewart said as he slipped his arms back into the damp white button-up. His necktie was in his pocket.

They were about ten minutes from shore at normal speed and would double the time on the water with the pace James set. He watched the sonar readout as much as the open water. They'd gone about fifteen minutes when he eased up on the throttle and frowned at the image there in greens and grey.

"There's something down there," he said, almost whispered it. "Has to be fifteen, maybe twenty feet long." He brought the throttle to neutral and killed the engine. They weren't on top of the shape, but pretty near. "I've never seen a fish that shape."

Stewart got behind him to look. "Damned if it isn't alligator shaped, huh?" And he *did* whisper this.

James shook his head gently. "I think you better get recording on your phone. I'd say we use the waterproof, but I'm not going in there, just in case we aren't both going crazy."

"What if we put it on a rope and lower it?"

The camera was about five hundred to replace, and dangling it there seemed like waving a baited hook, but… "If it eats it, we go splits on buying me a new one?"

"Yeah, no problem."

James rose from the chair and Stewart stepped to the bow of the boat to see if he could put eyes on the creature. While James dug into a storage compartment beneath the floor, Stewart watched the water, but saw nothing; neither had eyes on the sonar readout or the motions below. This was careless.

As if reeled in like a great fish, the massive gator leapt from the water and belly-slammed onto the deck only inches behind Stewart. The hull cracked and the boat immediately began to sink. James popped upright at the same moment Stewart got out half a scream. Two splashes followed, one right on the tail of the first and the latter being greater by at least tenfold. Despite the increasing incline as the boat began to cant, aching to snap in two, James struggled up to the bow. Bubbles began to rise and then Stewart's hands shot out, splashing a heartbeat before his head appeared. He wore a mask of terror.

"Did you see it?" Stewart shouted and then added, "Bring me in!"

"I'm sinking! We'll have to swim!" James tossed in the rope he'd intended to use for lowering the camera.

Stewart grabbed the rope, his eyes big as full moons. "No! Get me out of the wat—"

Great jaws came up on either side of him, rising to his abdomen, the mouth big enough to fit over Stewart's paddling legs. The jaws clenched and agony played on Stewart's face as his eyes bulged and his mouth stretched far enough to split at the corners of his lips.

"Hold on!" James shouted and jumped back around the side of the cabin to lever the rope. He began pulling with all he had, even as cold ocean water soaked his feet proving that when he did get Stewart up that it was only temporary.

The gator's teeth broke flesh and it began to ragdoll Stewart, but he never let go of the rope. He wailed and shook; his lifeline remained in his grip.

"Come on! Come on!" James groaned. The water was now up to his shins. He reefed with all he had and then some, splashing with each kick to recalibrate his footing against the incredible drag. "Come on!" His words barely registered above the raucous slashing and the burbling of his sinking ship. Then, slowly, slowly, he began reeling in the great weight on the end of the rope. "I got ya! I got ya!"

The splashing slowed. The rope had become plentiful on his end. Around the corning of the cabin came Stewart's face. He was printer paper pale but for his too red lips and greying tongue. His eyes were two dead bulbs gazing blankly as water splashed against them. The rope had wrapped around his forearms, but his hands were slack. Beneath his ribcage was a crimson mess of torn guts, stringy and sticky as seaweed.

"Dear God," James said and let go of the rope.

A big splash sounded on the far side of the cabin a second before the bow separated from the rest of the ship with an incredible crack. James looked to the shore—about one hundred yards—and then to a buoy—about fifteen yards. The buoy was an older model, one the hydro company had put in place to mark where the line went underwater. Its base was a squat circle about the size of a family sedan's hood. Above that was a steel ladder-like structure that rose maybe six feet. On top of that was a sensor of some sort that never stopped blinking a bright red light.

That blinking light suddenly looked like

salvation.

The boat disappeared beneath him and James immediately pushed himself for all he had, certain each kick was like ringing the gator's dinner bell. The splashing behind him was loud and close and his body nearly froze with terror as a steady whine played from his lips. In a blink, he arrived at the buoy. His hands slipped off the briny surface. He didn't dare look behind him. Scrambling, clawing, kicking, he managed to get himself onto the platform. Without pause, he climbed to the very top of the stubby ladder.

Finally, he looked back.

The gator was nowhere in sight and Stewart had sunk far enough that only his forehead bobbed above the surf. James stared at the head and the blackened water around it. His boat was a series of shadows in the moderately shallow waters. Eventually, only the tide moved and James caught his breath where he swayed, arms and legs vise-grip stiff. He decided that if the gator didn't come back for the rest of Stewart in the next mental-math ten minutes, he'd make a go for it to the shore.

He began counting to sixty. He got through three and a half times before the gator circled the buoy, eyes and nostrils above water, and then returned to Stewart's corpse for seconds.

Now's the time. The only time. Go! Go! Go while it's eating!

James couldn't make himself move and watched as the beast ate the insurance salesman and then spit out the rope like an errant roast tie left in the beef.

19

The family sat around the small, square dining table. Between them was the board game *Jumanji*. Everyone was having fun, but they'd been visibly tired since supper, as if someone had flipped a switch and now all were inching toward passing out. Carole gave George about two minutes of smiles before she suggested they head back to the hotel. Alexis was out on her feet, so, for a nice change, there were no arguments.

As Josie began clearing away the pieces and cards, the power cut out. "Uh oh," she said. "You have the number for the hotel?"

"Why?" Carole said.

"Because I have a generator and they don't— well, they do, but only covers the safety systems. So, if you go back, you'll be in the dark," Josie said as she fumbled blindly until she found the lighter she'd stashed in a bookshelf next to the dining table.

"We'll be going to bed, so…" Carole said.

"Sure, if the power's only out tonight, but call and see."

"Right," Carole said. She dialed as Josie made her way to the door and then outside. The wind had picked up and was blowing branches in a spooky kind of way. A voice in Carole's ear said hello and then without being asked said that yes, the power was out and no they didn't know when it would come back on. "Can I get into my room?" Carole asked. The doors used power locks with keycards.

"Yes, of course," Mandy Ng said. "Emergency power is up and if the full power isn't back on by eight, the generator is used to heat some of the kitchen equipment that doesn't already run on gas."

"Oh," Carole said.

An engine rumbled and the lights in Josie's cottage lit.

"I apologize for any inconvenience," Mandy said.

"Any word on what caused it?" Carole asked.

Josie stepped back in through the kitchen door. She went to the fridge and unplugged it—the food would make it until the morning without anything spoiling, cool as the night was.

"Since there's no storm, my guess is animals. Unfortunately, we'll likely have to wait until morning. The ferry service was down this evening, and all sailings are cancelled for tomorrow too. Both our local hydro employees are playing baseball. Someone will have to come via water taxi tomorrow," Mandy said.

"What luck," Carole said. "Well, okay."

"Your keycard will work," Mandy said. "Is there anything else?"

"No, I guess not." Carole hung up and looked at her mother. The cottage had only one bedroom. The couch pulled out, but that still meant sleeping two to two beds, and sometimes Josie snored something awful. "How about they camp out with you and I come back out in the morning?"

"Power's out then?" Josie said.

"Yes. And the hydro workers are playing baseball and the ferry service is cancelled for tomorrow," Carole said, audibly frustrated.

"You weren't leaving tomorrow anyway," Josie said and began rooting in drawers for candles. The fewer things plugged in, the longer the diesel in the generator lasted.

"I know, but they have to water taxi someone in to fix it. Meaning there won't be power for most of tomorrow. It's just…irritating," Carole said and had to resist stomping a foot. She needed to get to bed and much sooner than later.

"Can we go home? I mean can we go to bed?" Alexis said, rubbing her eyes.

"You're going to stay here. All I have to do is pull the bed out of the couch," Josie said.

"You have this under control?" Carole said. Josie waved her off. "You two all good to stay over?" she asked then, mostly of George. Like usual, he hadn't voiced an opinion one way or the other. George nodded. "I'll see you in the morning then. Have fun."

Once in the car and following the dark, dark path, a sense of relief washed over her. She hadn't had a kid break since Shane did what he had, and it was obvious she needed one. Too bad the water would be cooling in the hotel's heater or she would have really enjoyed a bath, a glass of wine from room service, and maybe something decadent, or at least as decadent as the Picture House Lodge menu dared to get.

Town looked dead under the mask of a powerless night. It felt right then like something forgotten and left to rot. She wheeled into the mostly empty hotel parking lot and was surprised when she stepped inside to discover people at the bar, drinking by candlelight, listening to soft rock on a radio. Mandy waved to her and she waved back. Among the men, she recognized the man who'd followed her off the ferry and she decided Ghost Clearing was like a pickle jar and they were all crammed together whether they liked it or not.

At her door, the card worked as promised and she used the face of her cellphone to carve a path to her bed. Once horizontal, she rolled side to side, lifted and shimmied away clothes before unhooking her bra and then stretching out in just her panties. She sighed after cocooning herself and was asleep within minutes.

20

The regulars and a handful of bored stragglers sat around the now cash-only bar. The candlelight was pleasant and soft but far from romantic given who all were in attendance. The topic had turned to the worst storms they'd each survived and how long they had to make it with the lights out. Mostly snowstorms, but a flood back in sixty-five took the cake for the longest outage.

Garth Crenshaw appeared as if from nowhere, entering the bar silently and emerging from the shadows into the candlelight. He'd been in earlier, and was supposed to meet James, but James hadn't shown, so Garth had left.

"James come in yet?" Garth said, his voice a little high and tense. There was fear there.

"No," Mandy said from behind the bar. "No sign of him?"

Garth shook his head. He looked like the crazy old man from slasher movies who has come to warn the kids. His eyes wide, his beard mostly gray, and his hair a little damp. "Hey, you, uh, scientist."

Denver nodded. "Yeah?"

"You were with him today; were you just around his traps?" Garth said.

"And the small island with the sea lion collective. Then we came back here and went to your house to get my rental car," Denver said. He had a single empty Moosehead bottle before him, label peeled away but clinging by a papery thread. "There was a man standing at the end of your lane when I left. I waved, but he seemed distracted or something. I don't know…he sold insurance with a tag still on his shirt…" Denver trailed.

"Has anyone seen Stewart?" Mandy said.

Like a shock to the room. Stewart wasn't there and he was almost always there come evening time. He'd have a thousand stories, mostly revolving around sales or lost sales; and tonight they all would have somehow started with a power outage.

"Uh oh," Janice said. She'd gone home after her shift but had come back once the power went out. Her husband and kids were off watching baseball and she really had nothing to do but go back into work as a customer and sip a couple beers, nod along with whatever was on the radio—currently it was Cutting Crew's *(I Just) Died in Your Arms Tonight*. She figured she might have it in her head for a week. That one seemed to play on a drill bit to the brainpan.

"Did you try him on the radio?" one man said.

"Was there a Mayday?" another said.

"I tried. Coast Guard at the mainland didn't observe any distress signals," Garth said.

"I know where Bob keeps the key to the search and rescue shed. We could take the boat out. Had one of those great big spotlights on it." Janice pushed from her seat as she said this.

Garth paused. The atmosphere in the room

suddenly matched the rhythm of his thoughtful breaths: weighty, calculating, assuming the worst but willing to seek out the best. "Yeah, maybe we better. I hope I'm not overreacting here," he said.

"Right, well, there's room for eight, but we better keep two spots. Garth, you can captain, right? I suck at it," Janice said.

"Maybe you better… I'm feeling a bit shaky right now." Garth sounded as if he felt guilty about it.

"I can do it," Todd Barber said. He was a quiet sort and had spent a good deal of his life as a deckhand on commercial fishing boats.

"Right, okay. Not drunk?" Janice said, wary. This was a lot of control and she wasn't exactly supposed to commandeer the rescue vessel. What were the chances something would happen the weekend when most of the townsfolk had gone to the mainland?

"I only sold him two Bud Lites," Mandy said, her words rising and falling as she nodded that he should be okay to captain.

"I had a Budweiser at lunch, too, if you're real worried. Three beers in about ten hours don't amount to much, but I'm guessing we aren't covered under insurance to take the boat," Todd said.

The word insurance seemed to shock the crowd into action and everyone pushed off their stools. With nothing else to do, no shows to miss on TV, forming a posse seemed downright logical.

"Whoa, not everybody. You, scientist, maybe you should come, and Garth, and Todd, maybe just one more. For muscle," Janice said.

The group looked to a man named Tony Silverman who stood at the end of the bar drinking a calorie-wise Michelob Ultra. He ran the local gym and for some unexplained reason detested baseball. "Sorry," he said. "I can't swim."

"Don't need to swim…better not need to," Garth said.

"I'll come," Henry Weight said. He was a handyman in the truest sense: concrete finishing, fixing boats, mowing lawns, touching up paintings, he did just about everything. His wife worked at Picture House Lodge but hadn't come in when the power was out—she opened tomorrow.

"I'll get out the short-wave," Mandy said, taking a candle and heading back around the wall to her office.

Denver followed the others silently, as if he wasn't sure what he could add to the search, though he wasn't going to argue being included. This vacation wasn't at all going how he'd planned when he'd explained it to his coworkers but he'd have plenty to talk about when he got home.

They took two vehicles to the emergency shed by the dock. Janice didn't go with them, instead ran the seven doors down to fetch the keys. In only a minute she met the headlight shined on the shed. It took just shy of ten minutes to have the door open and the rescue boat unmoored and moving—which was twice as long as it would've taken the rescue team. Of course, the rescue team had practiced this dance a hundred times, had performed it a half-dozen more in recent years when trouble had come brewing.

They raced out to Lion Island, zooming miles by the exhausted and terrified James South where he clung to a buoy for fear of being eaten by the world's biggest alligator.

21

The gator sat not twenty yards from the buoy, watching the blinking light, waiting for something to change. The light was a pulse belonging to a fleshy heat that was worth waiting for. But patience stretched only so long. The gator sprang from the rocky floor, its great clawed toes raking over the fortified hydro line. That fortified cover split, and the moment electricity met water, the breaker shorted on Picture Island. Three seconds later, it shorted on the mainland. The gator was about to crest the surf when the light, that red pulse of the meat, ceased blinking. Turning, the gator bumped the buoy as it changed direction. It heard the whimper of the hot-blooded meal hiding high up and wondered what the change meant.

The gator preferred the hot, hot human blood to anything it had eaten from the ocean. The meat had been more tender, richer. The gator curled back around to where it had sat, deciding right then to go for the figure atop the buoy. It surged before it leapt and snapped once, close, but as its foot put pressure on the base of the buoy and the ladder up top—along with the hot meat—rocked away from its mouth. A fresh whimper rang out. This one louder than the first. The waves created by the attack swayed the buoy, rocking it back and forth.

The gator spun and watched the hot meat dip close to the water and then shoot in the opposite direction, nearly crashing into the water on the far side.

The gator broke, trying to time the rocking motions, but it had grown lesser, and the gator snapped its jaws on air with an incredible *clank!* Another whine pierced the quiet of the ocean. The gator paused then and looked up at the hot meat. It couldn't stay there forever, nothing stayed put forever. The gator could wait.

It found a great crevice in the stone floor and nestled in. The meal it had eaten earlier was digesting nicely in its six stomachs. Outside appearance and aggressiveness, this gator had little in common with the Earthly creatures, past or present. It had different anatomy and different evolutionary patterns, despite coming from a world of oxygen and water and carbons.

The gator watched the hot meat until it began to doze. When it awoke, the sun had disappeared. Time was so different on this planet, though the giant gator had no way of knowing that. Though if it had looked in a mirror and marked its progression hourly, it could've noted exceptional—by Earth standards—growth. Soon enough it would reach maturity.

The hot meat remained clinging to the buoy, just out of reach. The gator was hungry again and was about to go for another shot at the meal when on the beach came the playful barks of two seals. The gator's eyes cut through the dark of night and zeroed in on the seals…and on something else. A plump creature on four legs, teasing the greasy black blobs. It was a similar color to the hot meat, and that alone made the new meal worth a shot.

Silently, the gator crept away from the buoy and onto the shore. Tide had gone out a ways and the gator stepped with the stealth of an assassin. The seals saw nothing and continued playing but the other creature—a white tail deer—stiffened and bolted for the rocky incline up the shore. It scrambled into the forest and the gator gave up its stealth, racing after the deer. The seals turned then and clumsily attempted escape, bouncing and rolling through the mucky shallows.

By the time the gator reached them, the deer had disappeared into the thick foliage and the seals had rolled and flopped into the water. There were options here, and the gator decided on one in the bush over two on the beach. It barreled up the ditch-like incline and followed the scent. Nearby, freshwater ran and momentarily distracted the gator—it could go for a drink, too. It swung around, wayward tail flung so violently an ages' dead elder spruce cracked and toppled onto the winding road, bringing with it two young birch bark trees.

The gator followed the road a while, picking up many scents and hearing multiple drinking options as it pushed deeper into the woods. This was better than the ocean. It would locate a pool to call home and feast on the huge bounty it smelled all around it. It would claim this place as its hunting grounds.

22

"I want to ask you something, George," Josie said. She'd just come inside from the backyard where she'd enjoyed a couple puffs from a joint and was finally feeling calm enough to ask what she thought Carole should've asked months ago.

George looked up from his cards. On the chair next to him, the old cat, Bozo, lay asleep. They'd been playing Old Maid by candlelight, wind-up radio offering up tinny hits from today and yesterday—currently some Bon Jovi.

"When your…when Shane killed himself, did you see him?" Josie said.

George looked at his cards some, as if they might reveal the secrets of the universe, or maybe an escape plan so that he could avoid this conversation. He shrugged, still not looking at Josie.

"This is important. Did you see him?"

George nodded.

"Will you tell me about it?"

The usually stoic George began breathing heavily, his eyes still on the cards, but now wet with tears. "He hung himself."

Josie exhaled a deep breath. "Yeah, I know."

"He put down plastic and pooped."

Josie swallowed then; this was something she didn't know to be true but had heard enough times to expect validity. "The body releases all its muscles after death and with him hanging like that…I guess he didn't want to make any extra trouble for Carole. Beyond what he had."

It wasn't easy, mustering sympathy for a man who'd do such a thing. She'd been raised to call such a thing cowardly, had *known* it to be cowardly most of her life, but lately, over the past ten years or so, she'd started to see all the ways she'd been lied to and in turn lied to others. Suicide had nothing to do with bravery or cowardice, it had to do with desperation and depression. She couldn't imagine a situation for herself where suicide seemed an easier option. She'd never, not in a million years, have the strength to carry it out.

"How come you didn't tell Carole? Something like that is traumatic for anyone, any age," Josie said.

George swiped his free hand beneath his running nose. "I told her and she didn't understand."

"You told her?"

"She said I couldn't see him, and she was sorry, but he was gone."

"When did you tell her?" Josie leaned in so close her loose hair was dangerously near to candleflame.

"The morning…when the cops came."

Josie backed up some and sighed. Age had given her the capacity for higher empathy—perhaps it was the weed because she knew enough ninnies who'd never shift their worldviews—and she imagined Carole's mindset at that traumatic moment; the day she found her husband dangling like a human pinata in their garage, plastic on the floor to catch whatever mess his body decided to make posthumously. She'd be scatterbrained at best.

"Carole would've been very upset and obviously didn't understand."

George steadied his jaw. "She never listens. She's nothing like my mom. Mom let us do stuff and pick out our clothes and didn't try to make us read books."

"You like reading comics?" Josie said, forcing the hint of a smile, trying to warm up the suddenly frosty room.

"Yeah, but usually she says, 'why don't you read a book?'"

"What about your sister?"

George looked at the foldout couch where Alexis lay. "She likes it because Carole buys her lots of clothes and lets her eat candy… Carole has more money than Mom and Dad."

Josie nodded. Even without a second income, Carole had really marked her place in the world. A big part of that was never having children of her own. Probably it was as if she had a savings account in her mind for just this scenario.

"Does what you saw in the garage make you feel bad?"

George shrugged. "I only saw his back and his legs" He paused for a few breaths and then said, "He did it because we came."

"No, don't say—"

"Carole makes us read and so I read what Shane

put in his—he had characters in every book that were sad and hated kids and had mean wives who tried to make them have kids and they never had kids before and then we came and then he killed himself," George said, rambling through a gasped breath that fell into a hitching sob.

Josie got up from her spot and hugged George. "It isn't your fault. All the bad luck is just that. Bad luck took your parents and bad luck put Shane in a spot he didn't like."

"Carole doesn't even care!"

"About you? That's not true, she loves—"

George tried to shove Josie away. "No! That Shane killed himself because we came to live with them."

"He didn't do that though," Josie gripped him tightly. "He killed himself because he'd broken down and, if it's like you say in his books, that he didn't know what to do, maybe about being married to Carole. It wasn't you at all, don't ever think that. Okay?"

George softened in her hands like cold dough coming to room temperature. "Okay."

"Do you believe me?" Josie spoke into his scalp.

"I guess so."

"Will you tell Carole all this and maybe you can work out some stuff?"

George was silent for twenty seconds before he said, "No. She wouldn't listen anyway."

Josie wasn't about to agree, but the kid had it right. "You know, you're quite astute for an eleven-year-old."

"Almost twelve."

"I know." Josie let go of George and shuffled to her side of the table but did not sit. "Say, how about we go light a little fire and have some s'mores?"

"What about Alexis?" George said.

"If she wakes up, we'll hear her and come get her."

It was eleven o'clock and Josie and George were wrapped up in flannel coats, plunked down by a creek, next to the hollow-centered tire rim, watching the flames grow high against the backdrop of a black, black night.

23

An overcast sky did nothing to help the search party scan the water. The ocean was a great black mat. They used radar and sonar. They'd found plenty of oceanic life, and the only potential sign of the boat was a large chunk of aluminum with foam padding wrapped around it. They'd fished it out and came to the all too troubling conclusion that it hadn't been floating all that long given that nothing clung to it.

"But how does his boat come apart out here? There's no weather for that?" Todd said. "I've seen a lot, but I've never seen a boat just fall apart on the water."

"A whale?" Janice said.

"When *Jaws* came out, another studio tried to jump on the coattails; remember there was a movie called *Orca?*" Henry said.

"This ain't a movie," Garth said. "But I think that's from our boat." He pointed at the rescued debris.

"Tide's heading out, guess we go closer to shore. If the boat went down on something closer—" Todd said.

Garth cut him off. "But why wouldn't he just swim in?"

"Could have a broken leg," Henry said. A

broken leg had become a good possibility in a sea of probable bad ones.

Garth huffed a long exhalation and then said, "All right, let's check closer to shore. But go slow, we don't want to go overtop of a wreck and miss it."

Todd had planned on it and started the engine. He pushed the throttle about a tenth of the way as Joyce played the high beam light over the calm waters. Within minutes, they started collecting more pieces of the missing boat, mostly fiberglass chunks. They were white, so was much of the boat James had taken out, then again, many boats were white. Most even.

"Must be coming up on shore, but where's the buoy light?" Todd said after they cut paths crisscrossing the water for more than two hours.

Janice knew where they were and swung the light hard to their left and shined it on the not-flashing light...and the man clinging to the ladder. "Holy, is that him?"

"Get away!" a hoarse scream carried from the direction of the buoy. "It's here!"

"Shit," Todd said and rather than taking heed, he punched the throttle down and buzzed along as close to the shallows as he dared. It was only seconds before he killed the gas and the boat stalled next to the buoy.

Garth stretched out, almost hanging by his toes, and grabbed onto the buoy ladder.

"Get away! It's here! It's here!" James screamed, the whites of his eyes glowing under the spotlight. His expression matched the words.

"It's okay, we're here," Garth said and reeled the buoy back toward the boat.

"It's here!" James said again.

"You're safe, you can let go now," Garth said, arms around his husband.

"You don't understand! There's a twenty-foot alligator and it fucking ate Stewart Russell in two bites!" James said after he let go and fell onto the deck of the rescue boat. "It's a monster and it's here!"

Todd and Henry looked at Denver like his higher education might give a clue as to what the man was talking about. "I don't know," he said, shoulders shrugging almost to his ears.

"Get us out of here!" James wailed and this time Todd did take his advice and started back to the pier and the shed where they could lock away the rescue boat.

"So, Stewart's dead?" Henry whispered.

24

The smells were so vibrant and the sounds so promising, but as the gator moved, one scent attracted above all other elements. Rotten, putrid, magnificent. The great beast cut into the woods, moving steadily uphill, suddenly ravenous for the creator of this smell. So much so that it knocked against trees and rocks, occasionally lost its footing, and twice had to regain its equilibrium after pitching over short drops. It snapped whole trees, created a rain of branches, and carved incredible divots in the forest floor. This raucous motion sent the local wildlife off in fits, breaking for known getaway trails, unaware that this new predator had become singularly minded.

That scent!

Suddenly it was close, so close. The gator slowed and began taking great but steady sips of the atmosphere through its nostrils. It honed and narrowed the target of the scent, tracking it to a hollow beneath a root structure and a great pile of grass and sticks. It stabbed its snout into the pile, rooting around until locating what it sought. Deftly, carefully, the gator pulled the bloated and maggoty corpse of a moose cow free of the hiding spot. It paused a moment, luxuriating in the meaty corruption. It opened its jaws and turned its head, but the moment before it snapped through the soft and fleshy morsel, a great growl played like an air raid siren.

The gator spun just as the seven-hundred-pound grizzly leapt onto the gator's back, swiping its fantastic claws against the leathery armor of its neck. The gator wailed and spun, snapping at air with great toothy clunks. The grizzly clung even as the massive beast rolled on and then off and then onto it again. The gator's tail swung, toppling three youngish trees and carving massive divots into the muddy floor. The grizzly bit down but did little damage. Though this was its first true test, the gator had come from a line of beasts overcoming creatures much, much bigger than the grizzly.

The gator bent down and sprung as high as it could while it turned in the air. It landed and bones snapped audibly, echoing through the otherwise still forest. Freed, the gator flipped sideways and snapped at the bear, catching a foreleg between its vise-like jaws. It clamped tighter and tighter; the grizzly cried out—making the pained sound instead forcing other animals to make the pained sound. The bones began to snap and the pelt tore. Hot blood showered into the gator's mouth and it dropped the severed limb. There was killing to do.

The hobbled bear attempted retreat, kicking in reverse, dragging its ass, not understanding that this was a pain it couldn't distance itself from. The gator pounced on the grizzly's back feet. With its remaining forepaw, the grizzly slashed, finding the thinner armor of the gator's abdomen and forcing out a green rain shower of otherworldly blood that sparkled on the sea of spiderwebbing lining the forest floor. Enough. The gator snapped its jaws as it jerked, almost pecking at the grizzly's head. Teeth sank beneath the bear's chin and behind the head. The resulting crunch was wet and promised death.

The decapitated grizzly flopped as tremendous spasms played throughout its body. The gator put its foot against the grizzly's chest until it finally quit moving, still poised to snap just in case. Once it knew the threat was no more, the gator returned to the moose cow and ate. Once done there, it ate all the soft bits of the grizzly, leaving its feet and head for scavengers to pick through. It spat some fur, but not all. There were few solids left; a bloodbath.

From there, the gator followed its ears, locating two creeks, before settling for a large and steamy hot spring pool. It floated and drank before it sank to the bottom and took a brief reprieve. There were new smells, ones from the water that had also been outside the water. The gator, once its energy was up again, would follow those hot meat scents until it located the source, but for now, sleep.

25

Carole hadn't always been so uptight. In college, she'd pissed away a huge chunk of her student loan and still had two months left of her first year's schooling to survive. The smart students applied for jobs at the start of the year. The somewhat smart students applied at the start of the semester. The not so smart students ran out of cash and applied for filled up positions months into classes when they and the potential employers all knew the students wouldn't be sticking around after exams. That was when she swallowed her pride and answered an advertisement in the local paper. The senior art classes needed models to pose, *18+* models. Carole was eighteen and she was broke and she was thin enough that she looked okay by magazine standards with her clothes off. As she sat, the point constantly going through her mind was, *if they could see me now.* The THEY of mention being anyone and everyone she'd known growing up, especially her parents.

Now, she lay in only her panties on the bed in the still dark hotel room, thinking about those days after a quickly forgotten dream put her on the subject. She imagined that old version of herself, the one Shane had fallen in love with, and she simply did not recognize her. This brought anxiety and guilt, but what had happened wasn't her fault. She'd done the right thing!

She reached over to the nightstand where she'd set her cellphone and lit the screen. She sighed. It had been a mistake to go to bed so early; no matter how tired she was, if she went to bed before eleven, she woke up almost exactly two hours later. It was a quarter to one and she was wide awake.

"Well, shit," she said and sat up.

Part of the draw to visiting Picture Island was the air out here and she decided this might be the only chance she had to take a quiet walk. She'd stick to the streets and be ready to bolt if another bear showed up, but she guessed she'd be fine. She'd read an article once that suggested nine out of ten bear attacks happened with a dog present, which meant that since she didn't have a dog, nothing was apt to bark a bear into action.

She dressed in fresh clothes from the closet and put her hair in a ponytail. She slipped into the hiking shoes she'd kept in the closet at home for more than a decade, bringing them out almost exclusively for Picture Island. With keycard in one hand and phone in the other hand, Carole departed her room and stepped into a quiet hallway, lit only by glow-in-the-dark stripes along the base of the walls.

She started toward the stairs and it wasn't long before she heard voices coming back to her. People were still up and at the bar, though the music had been turned off or perhaps the radio needed winding up. She considered stepping by them, but the main doors burst open and five men and a woman came in; they were damp and disheveled. One man leaned against two other men, looking like a boxer on the wrong end of a ten count.

"Is he okay?" Mandy said.

"Was Stewart not with him?" asked one of the men who'd stayed behind at the bar.

"Better get him some water and maybe something salty," Garth said.

"That fucking thing ate him," James said.

"What?" Tony said, rising instinctively, flexing for a fight, as if he might punch the mysterious *thing* to death.

"There's a monster gator out there and it fucking bit him in half and then tried to get me but I was on the buoy and when it stepped on the platform, I rocked out of reach, and when it tried to time me, it missed, then it gave up, but I saw it down there, waiting for me, but I wasn't getting down, not so that fucking thing could eat me, no way was I getting down, it fucking ate Stewart, bit him right in half like he was nothing and when I pulled him back it was just his chest and guts stringing out from beneath him, then I swam to the buoy while it was finishing Stewart like chomp chomp chomp and I got away but it would've had me and I—" James quit his urgent ramble for a breath before he slumped and accepted the cold glass of water from Mandy. She'd also brought over an individual tube of Pringles.

"A gator?" asked another man who'd stayed behind.

Mandy looked at Denver. His eyes rose and he registered her gaze. It took a moment by candlelight to read her expression, but then he got it. "No," he said. "Couldn't be...no."

"What if?" Mandy said, stepping around the other men to stand at Denver's side.

"Impossible." Denver frowned deeply and squinted, as if that pairing of actions might make his mind connect all the dots of this situation just a little bit faster. Create some sense from this nonsense.

"What if, though? I mean how did life get on Earth?" Mandy said.

"Adam and Eve?" Todd said.

Mandy ignored him, glancing at an approaching Carole before returning her attention to James. "How did it come?" she said again.

"Did you say gator?" Carole said.

James nodded. "Like a dinosaur. Biggest thing I ever saw."

"I heard that. Gators are dinosaurs," Henry said.

"Molecules...RNA," Denver said, keeping his conversation pinned to Mandy and not the others.

"And where did that stuff come from?" Mandy said, leading the horse to the trough.

"It came from—no, but it took four and a half billion years—" Denver started but was cut off.

"I heard Earth's only like eight thousand years old," Tony said.

Forgetting diplomacy and that this gym rat was massive, Denver said, "That's trying to make science conform to asinine Biblical fictions. It took four and a half billion years for the mutations and molecules to match up to what we see today."

"But those molecules were alive, frozen. They

land on Earth, thaw out and then…" Mandy trailed.

"I refuse to—" Denver said.

"The egg! You saw the shell pieces! You have them in your car! What if a whole pond were frozen and rocketed off a planet somehow, and it froze with an egg in it. The life in the egg was almost ready to come out and play, but then froze and was kept in…uh…" Mandy trailed, looking for the term.

"Suspended animation?" Janice said. The adjacent conversations had stalled.

"That's right! Then it thaws and it's like a great big alligator? It's far-fetched, but isn't that like a science thing? Once you eliminate the impossible, whatever's left, even if it's way out there, must be the answer?" Mandy said.

"Think that was Einstein," Todd said.

"Sherlock Holmes, sort of," Garth said. "And if James says it was a big gator, then that's what it was. If he says it ate Stewart, then that's what happened. If it came from…God knows where, then that's where it came from. The only thing I know is that a gator can go on land and in water, so if it has a taste for man, it'll soon be sniffing around here. Unless we stop it."

"How big you say it was?" Todd said.

"Twenty, twenty-five," James said. He was shivering with his hands between his thighs. "Can I have those?" He pointed an index finger to the Pringles can on the table.

Henry passed them over. "What you thinking?" he said.

"A gator skin that big would make an awful lot

of wallets…might be it's worth taking a peek, see if we can't put a couple rounds into it. Lots of swamp people hunt at night, don't know if that's for gators, but…" Todd said, leaving room for agreement.

Carole finally spoke. "You're going to shoot guns at night?"

"Only at the gator," Henry said.

"What if you miss and shoot into the woods?" Carole said, thinking her kids were in the woods. In the woods where a monstrous gator might be. "Holy God." She had to go out there and get them. She spun on her heels and charged back up the stairs, and then into her room for the car keys.

26

Denver was too baffled and curious to stay at the hotel while the wound-up group departed into the dark night with plans to meet at the harbor, armed and dangerous. Janice was the only woman with them, as Mandy stayed behind with a handful who either weren't up for the task of night hunting or simply weren't interested in playing hero. In the case of Garth, he was staying with James. Nothing was going to take him away.

While the others ran home to get their guns and flashlights, Denver collected his camera from the trunk. As he walked toward the harbor, he sent the same text message to two colleagues, meaning it, partly, as a joke:

If I don't make it back, it's because I've been eaten by a space gator

They'd almost certainly be asleep now, but this thing he was up to felt a hell of a lot more dangerous than the norm. A man was dead, torn in two according to the only surviving witness— though he was in obvious shock and what the man had described was a little tough to swallow.

A lifted truck passed him as he walked and then a Pontiac from the eighties that looked to be in collector's edition condition, though why anyone would preserve a 6000 LE was as big a mystery as the crushed crab trap. By the time Denver got to where the others had gathered, the discussion had settled into the idea of forming two groups. One would go on land and the other on the water.

"Never escape us then," Tony said and looked around for approval, catching a few nodding heads, which was apparently all that he needed.

Denver frowned at this group. They didn't have enough information to catch much of anything; and he still couldn't buy the idea of an alligator but said he'd like to join whoever captained a boat. It felt safer on the water; no matter what happened, people in a boat should only be shooting out of the boat. The men in the forest…who knew?

Within minutes, all the stragglers had come along, and the dozen members were split into two teams. Todd, Janice, Denver, and two other men would take the rescue boat, while Tony, Henry, and five other men, each carrying a rifle, would look for signs of the creature on the beach and into the forest, if necessary.

"Hope they don't kill each other," Janice whispered as she led them back into the rescue shed. She must've had an idea earlier that they'd need to do more because she hadn't wrapped the chain or fastened the thick padlock.

The water was black aside from the dulled grey reflection of the moon, shining meekly through the cloud cover. The waves shimmered on the breeze and the world seemed impossibly calm for someone to have been eaten in this water only hours earlier.

Todd steered them back to the general vicinity of the buoy while Janice worked the spotlight.

Nobody spoke for long stretches, and with each splash, Janice jerked the light around, hoping to catch a glimpse.

"If we see it, one of you better get a picture," Janice whispered. "Bob's going to be on edge about me taking this out."

"Thought you would've texted him by now?" Todd whispered back.

"Not yet," Janice said.

Denver lifted his camera just a little bit higher, had it a little more ready, as if he owed this stranger his best effort. *Don't lie to yourself; if you document this, you'll be the man who has discovered aliens with undeniable truth, and got it into the mainstream news. YOU!* The notion of this had him tingling all over—despite that he was still riding at about 90% certainty that this simply couldn't be happening.

But aliens. He truly believed the government had covered up contact, there were simply too many sightings and accounts to ignore, and not only from crackpots. He'd heard things from colleagues working in different fields of space, whispered things that might cost their careers if they'd said it too loudly. But with photographs and the shell pieces, he could be the *one*. He could be the guy.

Distantly, on the shore, the men of the other team could be heard whenever Todd stilled the throttle. It was then that Denver remembered enough of the guys from the bar had had more than a few drinks. Some seemed bound and bent on killing the time without electricity in a stupor. He looked back around the boat and discovered one of the *hunters* was asleep in his life jacket.

How bad an idea was this?

27

Felled trees crossed the road, big ones, and Carole sat there idling for five minutes wondering if someone was coming to fix this issue. Of course they weren't. It was the middle of the night and most of the town's population was away. She sent another text message to Josie to warn her, but nothing came back in return. Was her mother the type to even leave the phone on? She had no way of answering that question because she'd never thought to make note of it.

"How many things don't you notice?" she asked the night as she stepped out of the car. From the trunk, she plucked out the emergency kit; from it, she collected a flashlight and two C batteries—she'd heard that if you wanted batteries to last, you took them out of the underused item. She put the batteries into the light and the beam was strong, cutting bluely through the darkness. She closed the kit and then locked the car.

The road was totally dark and the night was mostly silent, until she heard the distant hollering of men. She didn't like that and picked up her pace. The hiking shoes—at least she'd been lucky enough to be wearing them—crunched and grated against the muddy gravel of the one and a half lane road. The trip in a vehicle was usually slow going, taking about half an hour, all told, but rarely did the speedometer rise above twenty miles an hour. This was only a slight comfort as she mentally tabulated the distance, so she tried to jog. The incline was gentle but steady and she found herself desperately winded after only a few minutes. She lowered her pace to a brisk walk.

Things in the trees rustled and branches swayed. She swung the light's beam back and forth. She really had no defense if an animal came upon her and she wasn't nearly as confident as she had been earlier when she'd planned to take a quiet stroll around town.

"Just keep going," she said and instantly had to stop.

On the road before her were two bear cubs, which she had an idea that meant mama bear wasn't far. She took a step back. From behind her, the trees rustled and a massive grizzly climbed up onto the road. Carole spun, shining the light on the beast, her other hand making a fist. The grizzly snorted and seemed to be licking its teeth beneath its great black gums. The blue of the light reflected off its greasy coat as it moved closer.

"Nice bear," Carole whispered and took a step in reverse.

The bear picked up pace and Carole took another backwards step. The bear growled and Carole stopped. The bear kept coming and Carole stiffened, closing her eyes. The stench permeating from this beast was incredible, awful. Its sniffing wet nose nudged at Carole's ribs. The sniffing drew higher and that wet nose touched her chin, clacking her teeth together, before stopping at her own nose. Carole opened her eyes and looked into the endless depths within the bear's gaze.

"I'm a mother, too. I get it," she whispered. "What do you think I'm doing out here?"

The grizzly sniffed once, twice, thrice and then roared in her face, spraying meaty saliva on a burning backdraft. Carole swayed. She closed her eyes. She tried to be steady.

"I'm no threat," she said. "I just want to reach my kids. I'm a mama, like you."

She waited and waited. The sniffing ceased and the stink lessened. When she eventually opened her eyes, only the bear's foul breath remained with her. She spun, slowly just to be sure, and discovered all three bears had departed. She used her sleeve and wiped her face and neck, pulled a few chunky bits out of her hair. There was no time to be revolted; in fact, the adrenaline offered up by the bear put a little more fuel in the fire.

Carole began jogging again, feeling better this time, though more desperate, as if she had to race that bear and all the trouble it could bring back to her   mother's   house.

28

Henry, or Handyman Henry as most of the townsfolk called him, wanted to be first and rushed ahead of the others as they made their way down onto the beach with their flashlights and weapons. Two guys had duct taped the lights to their rifles like bayonets, but Henry figured that would cause more trouble than it would help. First off, their aiming would be all messed up. Second off, they'd get tired pretty quickly of swinging a whole damned rifle when they could just be swinging the light.

The beach was rocky and that might've covered up tracks, but if this thing was even half as big as James had said, it must weigh a thousand pounds, maybe more. Movement of something that big, rocks or not, would leave a trail. But only if he knew exactly where to look. Instead of scanning the beach ahead, Henry shined his powerful flashlight on the water, looking for the buoy James had clung to.

Once he spotted it, the light dead as Stewart Russell, Henry picked up his pace, scanning the beach between him and the buoy for anything untoward. Not for a second did he think he'd stumble upon such a catch, not one so big, hunting was never like that—he also never entertained the idea that he might be the prey in this situation. He nearly rushed by what he sought but once the carved line took root in his head, he spun, marring the evidence with his bootheels. He shined the light up the short but steep bank into the woods. The scrape of this thing's movements cut a massive swatch into the woods. Above, maybe thirty feet from where he stood, a glinting light came back to him and he aimed the rifle.

The question: was this eyeshine?

He played the light gently through the thick foliage as the other men came up the beach, chatting drunkenly, as if they'd never been hunting and didn't know quiet was one of the necessary elements to bagging a kill. They did however play a halfway useful role here. Had that shine been eyeshine from an animal, the sound of the men would've had it moving. Nothing was apt to sit there and wait for a top of the food chain predator to come along and take it out.

"Here," he said and lowered his rifle and the beam of his light. Quickly, he decided the rise was passable and leaned forward. He engaged the safety and tossed his rifle up onto the road above.

"What you got?" Tony said, breathing heavily from running to catch up.

"It went this way," Henry said and began to climb the muddy slope. Once up, he shined his light on the felled trees and then on the car parked just beyond them. It wasn't a local car, he knew the entire damned population and what each of them drove, even knew what they had in storage and only brought out for special occasions.

"Holy, it knock down those trees?" Tony said.

Henry hadn't thought that far ahead and shined the light along the road, leading back to the cracked and splintered stumps. "Must've," he said. He scanned. About fifty paces to his left, something big had cut through the trees once again, heading up the hill.

"Geez, could it really?" Tony said.

"I think it did and I think you better tell those guys to shut the hell up," Henry said.

"Why me?" Tony said.

"'Cause you're big as a house and they'll listen to you," Henry said and started up the road, trailing the next access point through the trees.

He shined the light and was in awe of the oddity of this thing's movements. It was as if it pinballed off trees, indifferent to them. It had to have been in a hurry.

"You guys, come on, but we got to be quiet. We're getting real' close and don't want it startled," Tony said from a ways back.

It would only last a little while, so Henry started up rather than waiting.

"Better text the guys in the boat," someone said.

Tony gave him a "Shh!"

Henry shook his head, drinking in the motions of something he wasn't close to comprehending.

29

The line for cotton candy was taking forever and George bounced from foot to foot, holding his crotch with both hands, clutching two dollars in cash in one of those hands. Nobody seemed to notice him, nobody took pity and let him cut. The line behind him was now going on forever. The piss was beginning to sting and despite being utterly ravenous, George bolted from line. He cut through the sea of people much taller than him and to the long aluminum trailer with the urinal trough.

It stank awfully in the trailer and something had clogged the trough. The deep yellow liquid was sloshing in waves, nearly creeping over the lip with every footfall of the numerous large men around him. George had no time to be disgusted and moseyed up to the trough and unzipped. Once the flow started, it was magnificent.

George opened his eyes and nearly screamed. His hand went down his shorts. Dry. It wouldn't remain that way. He bounced from the spongy fold-out mattress and looked around the near total darkness of the cottage. All he could make out was the moonlight coming through the back door. He didn't remember how to get to the toilet, so outside would have to do.

He moved with his hands out, like a tightrope

walker. He bumped his knee once and his hip once but did so quietly. Upon reaching the door, he was able to speed up—and, boy, he needed to speed up. He had his shorts down at the front even before his feet touched grass. He directed himself toward the trees—somewhere less travelled was good enough right now—and let the flow fly. He sighed long and deeply. This felt even better than the fair dream that was quickly fleeting and would disappear inside a minute. He finished and shook. Shook again.

Tree branches snapped to his left. Those sounds were pretty close, but how close, he had no way of telling. Everything on this island was different from life in the city. Life in the city was predictable, reliable, the rules were laid out and everyone followed them. On the island, nature made the rules, even if people pretended it was otherwise. There were hardly any signs or markers. The roads were rough and old. The danged power went out and didn't come back on.

George turned; the grass was rough between his toes. The night air was chilly. The atmosphere was fresh but tainted. He inhaled deeply, wondering if his piss stank or was it something else. Another branch broke. George held his breath. That one was close, too close.

Snap!

George bolted for the door. His feet thumped with damp smacks against the aged wood of the back porch. His right foot skidded as his left foot slipped out from beneath him when he stepped in a small puddle about a foot from the potted marijuana plants.

Snap!

Screech!

George gasped and watched the empty sky above him, certain something was coming, maybe even that bear from earlier. That grizzly bear from the hotel garbage maybe.

Squee! Squee!

The sound was small and more off-putting than frightening. George rolled to his hands and knees and looked out at the lawn. The cloud cover had lessened and he saw clearly the shiny snake with golden markings with something smaller than a baseball in its mouth. George watched a while longer as the hapless efforts of the mouse were thwarted with visible ease by the hungry snake.

Snap!

This came from another direction. He heard voices then. Men's voices. That was a scary thought. There should be no unknown voices out here. He hurried into the cottage and closed the door quietly. He pawed around until he found the deadbolt and spun it closed. He didn't know if the front door was locked, but knowing Josie, he doubted it. Carole had said she didn't used to be this easygoing, that age had changed her. He'd also heard Carole on the phone once calling her mother a stoner, saying she'd become the Big Lebowski. George knew about *The Big Lebowski* movie from a friend, back when he'd had good, close friends and his parents were still alive. His friend had an older sister and she made them watch it one night when she was babysitting.

George bumped into a dining chair, screeching it a few inches across the floor. He waited to hear if he'd awoken Josie—he prayed internally that he had; she should know about men's voices not too far away. No sounds came from her bedroom aside from her snoring and he pushed the yawning bathroom door halfway closed in order to get to the deadbolt on the front door. He paused there, huffing at the bathroom's location. The cottage was tiny and it had maybe five doors total, he could've easily found his way to the toilet.

A simple thought once the pressure was off.

He shuffled back to the living room and climbed in next to his sister. He was most of the way to dreamland when more branches snapped outside and more voices joined them, so rather than getting up, his mind incorporated them. He was at school. People were yelling. Those snaps were simply locker doors.

30

Janice and Todd led the way with arms drawn. Denver had the best light, so he was only a half-step behind them. The man who'd fallen asleep in the boat didn't tag along once they'd docked and began the land search. The final man followed silently. He'd said hardly anything at all, not even when they'd been at the bar and the booze was fresh in his system. To Denver, not knowing his name gave his presence an ominous vibe, and that vibe was accentuated by the alarming markings on the shore that led up into the woods.

"If this is a gator…sheesh, it'd have to stand six feet tall. At least," Todd said.

"Have you fished for alligators before?" Denver asked.

"Called baiting, and no. That don't mean I don't know a thing or two," Todd said.

"I didn't mean to suggest—" Denver began.

"Suppose we ought to follow," Janice said, cutting him off.

"Right, unless the professor here has any other ideas?" Todd said.

Denver bit down a retort. This was becoming a long and trying day, and his being the voice of logic went against most of the evidence presented and their urgency to believe something crazy. He shined his light up the embankment until it was his turn to climb. Up on the road, the trail of the beast was clear. The cloud cover had dissipated and the half-moon revealed the way like it was gold at the end of a rainbow.

As they walked, stomped, sidled into the brush, Denver tried to imagine looking at a beast that stood eye-to-eye with him, but also stretched out twenty feet, or more, beyond that. What they should be doing is calling in for help. This animal was a significant find, no matter where it had originated. It was the kind of find that might put him on magazine covers…if he managed to keep it alive, and he supposed, to keep from being eaten.

"You don't know what this is," he whispered.

"What's that?" Janice said. She was just ahead of him, leading the single-file line. She had her rifle pointed to the ground and Denver hoped to hell Todd Barber was doing the same behind him.

"Nothing," Denver said.

Distantly, voices echoed, trailing like a double exposure, and then the first shot rang out.

"Uh oh," Janice said and picked up the pace.

31

It took Henry a moment to understand what he was looking at. At first, he'd thought a grizzly had dug a hole and then crouched in it, perhaps falling asleep with only its head aboveground after a big and bloody meal. But no. It was just a head, and that blood—the red stuff anyway; that sort of glowing green stuff that had coated what appeared to be a wolf spider colony, who knew what that was—had belonged to the bear. And that bear had been big, according to the size of what remained. Big enough that it had no predators that could've possibly done this, especially not before the blood dried on the forest floor. Perhaps, given enough time, something might pick a bear that clean after it's bested. But to munch that much in a sitting…James hadn't lost his mind. This thing was an undeniable monster.

"Be ready, this thing's a killer," Henry said.

"Holy shit," Tony said, coming up from behind him.

"Christ," Kirk Esposito said; he was the town's barber, and he carried a .30-60 rifle painted in green shades of camouflage and a crappy plastic flashlight that refused to stay lit.

"No more talking. Might be close," Henry said and led the way deeper into the woods.

They crossed the road once more, avoiding its meandering path actually saved them a good deal of time; had they waited a couple minutes or been later to the trail, they would've seen Carole McNaughton's flashlight cut through the gloom.

"Not far from Josie's place," Gil Parent said. He was another fisherman but had a drinking problem and couldn't afford to go watch baseball on the mainland. He carried a .22 rifle that was twice his age and felt wholly underwhelming given the evidence presented to them so far.

"Shut up," Todd hissed and then looked to Henry for approval.

Henry gave a curt nod before carrying on. They were indeed near Josie Kincaid's cottage, but they were closer yet to the hot springs. The ground beneath their feet became slick and muddy, the trail of the creature suddenly hard to miss.

Henry waved the guys over and pointed toward where the beast's route should be. "Impossible to climb and be ready," he whispered. "We take the road and pick the trail up again after."

"You think it's up there?" Gil said.

Henry shook his head. "No. I doubt it is. My guess, it's headed for Toenail Lake."

"How's it know where—?" Kirk started.

"Shh, move," Tony said.

Henry stepped slowly and carefully. Kirk's ˙ ~uestion had him wondering why he ˙ ɔr, or whatever it was, wasn't very patch of brush. Because it ι step on its tail and never notice ɪnd and bit his body off, leaving only his head, just like it must've done to the grizzly. This nearly made him stop; fear of looking like a coward kept him going.

Once onto the road, he felt a little better with the solid, man-carved ground underfoot. The view was clearer and the chances of anything jumping out at them seemed lesser, and if something jumped out, they'd have a second or two, assumedly, to take care of business.

Henry lifted his rifle in new anticipation. When the hot spring came into view, it was almost a letdown that the giant gator wasn't perched on the lip of one of the pools, just waiting to be shot. None of the pools seemed big enough, though each had a shallow side and a deep side, so it was possible…but no. That didn't make sense. Henry stepped over to the trail they'd stopped following for those short minutes and he tried to pick it up anew. The ground was rocky and the markings weren't nearly so clear, but Henry had no doubt that he'd locate the trail again, beyond the pools.

He waved for the others to follow. They did, slowly, Gil lollygagging in the rear, running his hand along the surf of the hot water of the first pool. The warmth was nice, reassuring somehow. He gave a little splash at Kirk and Kirk spun, making a face at him. Gil grinned; he was still a good sum drunk. He rounded the pool while letting his hand dip back into the steamy water.

Kirk spun at the next splash, ready to say something, but the man was gone. The flashlight and rifle were on the ground and the pool w· aflutter with waves. "Hold up," he said.

"Shh," Tony said.

Kirk frowned, leaning over the pool that now seemed a little darker in hue than it had before. Bubbles rose and he leaned closer. "Gil, you better not be play—ahh!"

From out of the pool leapt the great beast, grabbing Kirk by the torso and carting him to the next pool before disappearing below.

"Geez. Geez," Tony mumbled and then began firing into the second pool, one shot after another.

Henry began jerking around, looking for a target. He spotted one when something popped up and bobbed on the water in the first pool. Gil's ruined corpse accepted each panicked shot, making his limbs thrash and dance, the water splash and sway.

Tony quickly ran out of ammunition and began fumbling in his pocket for more. Henry saw what he'd hit and his gut sank. He aimed at the second pool, waiting, waiting. Bubbles rose steadily with the heat, but then larger bubbles began to come up. He tensed in anticipation.

The gator leapt and Henry nailed it twice, but slowed it none at all. Tony's huge frame was closer and the gator closed its fantastic jaws over him. Henry fired again. Hit. Again. Hit. The gator lifted Tony and shook him like a maraca, his snapping bones playing the role of the pebbles while he screamed the wordless lyrics of agony. Henry squeezed the trigger. It clicked.

The gator tilted its incredible head back, began chewing and swallowing simultaneously. It had its eyes on Henry from where it perched on the lip of a pool. Its snout reached as high as some of the trees when it tilted to swallow more human meat. It was right then that Henry understood that if anything was a predator and anything was prey, he'd had the order wrong when they stepped out onto that beach and followed this thing's trail.

He turned and bolted for the road. There was only one building anywhere near there and they'd damn well better let him inside.

32

Alexis was the first to rise after hearing the shots. Through the gloomy cottage, she tiptoed until she reached Josie's door. She didn't knock. She turned the knob and entered, finding the space twice as dark in there, almost pure black but for the line next to the heavy drape over the window. Alexis stepped forward until she felt bed. She reached out then and grabbed Josie's foot.

Josie sat bolt upright and shouted, "What in the fuck!" She then hit a battery light and laughed upon seeing the little girl at the end of the bed.

"There's something banging outside," Alexis whispered.

Josie almost spoke again, but then heard back-to-back rounds go off all too near. She kicked out from beneath the sheets in her ankle length nightie. Screams rang out and suddenly George was in the doorway squinting into the bedroom.

"It's okay, just…how about you stay in here and I go check out what's happening," Josie said.

George nodded.

"I'm scared," Alexis said.

George stepped deeper into the room and took her hand.

"That's a good boy," Josie said as she passed them by, patting George's shoulder twice. She reached the door and wondered who had locked it, but ignored the question and hurried out to the shed. Within seconds, the generator was rumbling. She ran back and flicked the kitchen light switch. "You stay put 'til I come back." She then went and closed the bedroom door and went to retrieve her rifle from the cupboard.

Bozo was awakened by the late-night activity and headbutted Josie's elbow. Josie ignored the cat, too busy loading the four rounds into the magazine and one in the hole. Bozo bopped against her legs and then put a cold nose and some tickling whiskers across her toes.

"Will you take a hike!" Josie said and Bozo scurried off.

She set the rifle aside and bent to retrieve the handgun. Perhaps she was being paranoid, but what were rifle shots doing going off in the middle of the night, and way up here? There was no good excuse she could think of, and what about the screaming? Nope. It would be one thing if she didn't have these kids here, but she did and if something happened… She loaded ten rounds into the magazine and put one in the hole. She took the rifle and handgun to the back door and discovered someone had locked this door too. The question of who was unimportant, fleeting. She grabbed her flashlight and left the handgun on the shelf next to the door. She knew where it was if a pinch came upon her.

Aiming into the night, light cradled beneath the rifle's barrel, she scanned the yard. Cracks and shouting, animalistic grunts and tree branches snapping. The sounds were coming from further up the hill. Possibly from the hot springs.

She stepped back inside and closed the door. The bolt sank home and she crossed the room, leaving behind the loaded handgun. She got to the kitchen. She opened-up the door and stepped out. She stared into the darkness of her front yard. The noises had quieted, but a different kind of noise approached. She aimed the rifle at the sound and waited. Light flashed, rocking up and down, slashing blue lines through the night. A shadowy figure appeared. In that moment, Josie applied about half the necessary pressure to fire against the trigger. Not sure. Not quite. The light danced and bounced and everything about the figure approaching remained in the dark.

"What…it's…me," Carole said, breathlessly.

Josie very nearly squeezed through at the sound of her voice on impulse, but she didn't. Instead, she lowered the rifle. "What's going on out here?" she said.

"Some…kind…of…animal," she said.

"Animal? Like a bear?" Josie said.

Carole stumbled forward and leaned on Josie. "It…came…from…" She swallowed and a fresh scream rang out. This one sounded almost like a word.

"Let's get inside," Josie said.

Carole went first and Josie locked the door behind them. Josie then pulled out a chair for Carole to sit down. She did. She looked downright whooped.

"Now, tell me," Josie said.

"There was a meteorite." Carole swallowed. The

resulting sound was dry and sticky. Josie went to the fridge and grabbed a bottle of Miller Genuine Draft. One-handedly, she popped the top off using the steel ribbon on the lip of her counter. She handed over the beer. "Thanks," Carole said and drank down half of it. "The meteorite had a massive alligator in it and now it's in the forest. Or something. Only one man saw it, but he didn't look good."

Josie scrunched her face. "What?"

George stepped out of the bedroom. He nodded.

"George even said. Holy cow, George even said, and I didn't put that together!" Carole said. She was shaking. "It killed a man, and now it might be in the woods. There were gunshots! They were hunting it, but then I heard men shouting and screaming."

Josie nodded. This was the part of the story she could swallow because she'd experienced it herself. The other part, well…

"Carole?" Alexis said, tears in the word.

Carole set the beer on the table and stood. She nearly fell, her legs gone to rubber, but she managed to stay upright and halve the distance between them before she embraced the girl rushing into her arms. "It's going to be okay," Carole said into Alexis' scalp, and then kissed her.

"We're all here. We're safe now. Nothing—" Josie started, but a muddy palm slapped against the glass of the front door a moment before a sunburnt face appeared.

"Let me in!" Henry the Handyman shouted. "Goddammit! You gotta let me in!"

33

Todd and Janice started running once they realized where the cries were coming from thanks to a background vocal of splashing water. That close, there was only one place water would be splashing with that much force, so they stuck to the road the moment it presented itself an option. Denver didn't have a weapon and didn't care for the sounds of violence ahead. Unintentionally, his strides shrank and he decreased speed. Almost immediately, he was looking at everyone's backs, watching their footfalls carry them into disaster. This was the smart move.

Maybe if he had more stake in this situation, if he knew or cared about the people who'd gone to hunt and kill this animal. An animal with limited capacity for thought—likely—one that didn't really understand its actions. Nature was nature and nature dictated most things.

By the time Denver reached the steamy hot springs, his group had begun cutting back through the woods and the sun was starting to rise, though offered only a tepid red glow in the distant east. He trailed in after them, careful that he didn't get too close.

Shots rang out and he picked up the pace, suddenly afraid that he was about to be caught without the protection of those he'd come with.

What if there were two creatures? Or, what if a bear cornered him?

He began looking into the trees—how many videos had he seen of bears in trees? "Dammit. Dammit," he said as he jogged until he came into a clearing.

Janice and the quiet man were side-by-side, aiming at a beast that had to stand six-five. Its length was incredible, and its speed and dexterity were inexplicable for something that big and covered in weighty armor. The shots rang out and all seemed to hit the beast, nestling into its leather body, but doing nothing to hurt it.

The gator—and Denver saw without doubt that until dissection and proof otherwise, that this beast would indeed be labelled a gator—bent at the knees and pounced forward. Todd had no chance to get out of the way and was flattened by the intense force. Janice and the quiet man continued firing until they had to reload.

"Are we doing anything?" Janice said, frantic, terrified.

The quiet man replied in a voice so high-pitched only dogs and bats were apt to appreciate it fully. "I don't know!"

Denver looked to the trees again after letting his eyes fall on the mess that had once been a fisherman name Todd Barber. The gator used its front teeth to wrench Todd's guts out in long stringy mouthfuls. Todd swatted at it with flimsy swings until the gator took another bite.

Janice had her weapon loaded and fired again.

Denver found what he was looking for. Janice fired another round as the quiet man shrieked in frustration at his rifle. Denver was halfway up a fortuitously climbable tree and watched. He killed his light and clung on for life.

The gator spun then, slamming its tail in a mace-like arc, driving the quiet man into Janice before he crumbled to the ground while Janice's body took flight. Her head and arms were thrown backward with an audible, gut wrenching snap. The tail followed through and nailed the trunk of the tree where Denver had hidden. He toppled into the action, eyes squeezed tight, his insides rollercoastering in a chaotic frenzy as the tree pitched with a series of cracks and snaps.

Denver opened his eyes. The wind had been knocked out of him and it probably prolonged his life. He was face to face with Janice, but his chest was against her back—her head had been spun. Had he any air at all, he would've screamed.

The gator grabbed the quiet man, who'd been hanging by a thread, and tossed him into the air. He cartwheeled and landed on his head with a fantastic set of crunches. Denver gasped and closed his eyes. He couldn't watch this. It was simply too much. He was no hunter, no warrior, not even a survivor. He looked at stars and math equations. All he wanted was a simple damned meteorite and now he had this. Even if he did make it out, would he recover from touching noses with a woman who had her head on backward?

And making it out, did that mean lying there or getting up and getting moving?

34

Josie didn't move right away. The shock of seeing the disheveled, dirty man at the door disabled her motor functions.

"Let me in!" Henry shouted after furiously turning the knob. "Goddammit, Josie! It's me, Henry!"

Carole squeezed Alexis tight to her chest, taking a step back as she did so. They bumped into George and he started away, moving with blind, plodding steps. He didn't stop until his shoulders touched the rear doorframe and the shelf. He jumped and spun, afraid he'd gone so far that he bumped into the gator that had somehow come to hide in the cottage.

"Please!" Henry whined. He smacked his palm six times against the glass. The final strike sent a spider web crack streaking toward the cocking within the frame. A noise stole his attention before he could punch out the glass and he turned. "Jesus! Jesus!"

Josie gasped, her body coming to. "Henry?" she said.

"Don't let him in!" Carole said.

Josie looked at her daughter with something like disgust in her expression and spun the deadbolt.

"Jesus! Let me in!" Henry screamed, facing the

yard.

Josie swung open the door and yanked the man inside just as a great flash of green, yellow, and black flew by the opening, swinging its tail through the siding, through the bones of the cottage's framework, and the drywall within. Dishes flew. The table toppled. Old construction dust flew. Carole's half-finished MGD fell onto the floor, spinning and foaming, vomiting a slow froth of white, white foam. The front porch crashed through, leaving only a splintered mess and an angry gator.

"Back door!" Josie shouted, scrambling to get out from beneath Henry.

The incredible tail had nailed his ankle, detaching his foot from his leg, though not tearing through his sock or pants. He didn't scream until he tried to rise.

"Go! Off!" Josie shouted, pushing him.

From amid the gloom, the gator's snout appeared and the beast launched into the kitchen, blowing out the door like it was made of toothpicks and loose straw. Josie grabbed for Henry's shoulders when the snout cranked sideways and bit into him.

"No! No!" Henry cried stupidly as he gawked at the creature.

"Let him go!" Josie shouted, yanking to no avail.

When he began hacking great bursts of blood, she let go and followed Carole and the kids out the back door. Carole and George were on the roof, they each had one of Alexis' arms and were pulling her up from the final piece of the trellis Josie had mounted on the wall just that spring. Josie put her hands on the highest rung she could reach. Her feet went up to the first and then second level.

"Come on, Mom!" Carole shouted.

"I wanna go home," Alexis whined.

George was reaching for Josie, trying to help.

Thumps rang into the night a moment before the rear wall of the cottage blew out on a cloud of splinters and sawdust. The gator passed long through and was skidding down the damp hill toward the firepit. Josie fell, but those on the roof remained upright, despite the rocking. She was bloodied but not badly hurt and pushed to her feet. The rifle was in the cottage still, so she hoped, and if she could just get it, she'd blow a hole the size of a baseball in this big bad beast.

"Where you going?" Carole shouted, cradling Alexis who was wailing steadily.

"Rifle," Josie said and then broke into a hobbled run, through the busted wall and into her living room. Splinters and nails slipped into her feet and she stumbled several times. "Ow, God. Ow."

The gator had its bearings and started a quick chase up the hill. If it had seen the hot meat packets on the rooftop, it was paying them no mind. Not yet anyway. It ran, swinging in a semi-straight-legged trot like an overlarge Komodo dragon. It was in the house far too quickly.

"Run!" George shouted and broke across the roof to the front of the house.

Josie snatched the rifle up from beneath what remained of Henry's right arm. She leapt through the door, falling heavily when a spike of wood drove up through her foot. There'd be time for pain later, if she survived. She got to a foot and a heel and started in reverse along the cool damp grass. She fired once.

"Come on, you sonofabitch," she growled, firing a second round.

The gator leapt into view and put the sum of its weight on Josie, snapping all of her ribs simultaneously and ejecting her guts and bowels out her anus while sending her lungs, heart, and throat out her mouth.

"No!" George shouted, pulling the .22 handgun he'd grabbed from the shelf out of his pocket and leaping off the roof and onto the gator's back.

It instantly began bucking, but his empty hand had been in a fist when he jumped and remained that way, lodged beneath one of the plates of thick armor. The gator stopped then and did a roll. George missed the brunt of the weight thanks to a soft lawn and a pliable body.

"Uh oh," a voice said from in front of George and the gator, a sound much closer than the cries of Alexis and Carole still on the roof.

Denver Jones lifted the pilfered rifle and aimed.

The gator burst forward, its head tilting so it could snap on the next delicious offering. George still had the little gun—puny, useless, little gun… He thought of *Unexpected*. The gator in the story he'd read had fallen into molten lead, but rather than burning up, the lead stiffened its already fantastic armor. The only way to stop it had been to…

Denver squeezed the trigger over and over, discovering but not registering that Janice had spent all her ammunition. He was screaming as he did so.

George's gun hand snaked beneath the armor at the beast's head just as it began to close its teeth on Denver. He fired once, and again, and again. He put four rounds into the creature and would've kept firing, but his hand lost the ability to squeeze through.

It didn't matter.

The clever attack stopped the beast cold.

35

James South was the first in line to volunteer to help bring the beast down the hill and into town. He'd suggested they do it in pieces and cut it up on the spot. Denver had made up a story about criminal liability when destroying an endangered species. Even just the remains. By lunchtime, the ten volunteers, using a series of strapped tarps, managed to heft the beast onto a trailer, and then to bring that trailer down to the Ghost Clearing Fishery's chilled shed.

A water taxi arrived before lunch and Stacy Brune, reporter, was running wild, kicking himself for missing the island's most exciting day in the history of the written word. A hydro worker was also on that taxi, though when he saw the extent of the damage, he apologized and headed back to the mainland. That line would take a team.

By suppertime, Stacy had documented the events with his camera—both shots and film—and had recorded more than a dozen eyewitness accounts. This was going to be the scoop of the century. He called ahead and the ferry company thought they'd have the ferry running again for tomorrow's evening sailings, which wasn't good enough for Stacy. He decided he'd spend the night getting all the information he could and take a water taxi to the mainland come morning—he'd have to pay the taxi both ways, but the footage and shots he had were nothing short of gold, the firsthand accounts of the events were platinum on top. He could've shrunk the files and shared them on a server, but it would've taken forever and what was a day when he was the only professional game in town?

Mandy, Garth, and James took turns snapping shots of those who remained and were interested, sitting on the giant gator or lying next to it while one of them climbed a ladder for a bird's eye. Other people got ready to bury loved ones, even more yet simply mourned for their town. The ball tournament was over; the Ghost Clearing Bears had won, but they, nor the booster club, could get home until the ferry was running.

Carole mourned for her mother. Alexis mourned for her sort of grandmother. George mourned for the first person who'd ever listened to him in an adult way. They were going to bury what was left of Josie as soon as they could and then leave the island forever. "If I never see this place again it'll be too soon," Carole said, and Alexis gave her a pouty face and a nodding head. George had Bozo in a carrier and looked at Carole in a way that she wouldn't dare tell him he couldn't keep the cat.

A little after eight o'clock that night, James locked the door they'd jimmied open to enter the Ghost Clearing Fishery's shed. At a quarter to one the following morning, three drunken teenagers climbed into the fishery through a window and shot video of themselves, mostly humping the beast.

A beast with a brain not in its skull, but in a

thick casing at the base of its neck. A beast from a species that had survived as an apex predator on its planet for more than one hundred thousand generations. A beast with built-in systems to protect it, to conserve energy, to shrink its life force until it was healthy enough to move safely— as-needed hibernating. A beast that looked like a pre-historic relative to an alligator but was not. A beast that existed in time differently from all other living beings on Earth. A beast that had reached maturity as it recovered from the tremendous blow to its skull that vibrated against the most vital of vital organs but did no irreconcilable damage to them.

"Kiss me, baby," said a young woman with vodka and vomit on her breath as she smooched the gator's snout. "Love me, baby," she added and closed her eyes. She was so into it and so drunk— they were all so drunk—that she didn't notice eyes opening or a chest rising to fill a set of rebooted lungs.

Check out other great
Cryptid Novels!

Hunter Shea
LOCH NESS REVENGE

Deep in the murky waters of Loch Ness, the creature known as Nessie has returned. Twins Natalie and Austin McQueen watched in horror as their parents were devoured by the world's most infamous lake monster. Two decades later, it's their turn to hunt the legend. But what lurks in the Loch is not what they expected. Nessie is devouring everything in and around the Loch, and it's not alone. Hell has come to the Scottish Highlands. In a fierce battle between man and monster, the world may never be the same. Praise for THEY RISE : "Outrageous, balls to the wall...made me yearn for 3D glasses and a tub of popcorn, extra butter!" – The Eyes of Madness "A fast-paced, gore-heavy splatter fest of sharksploitation." The Werd "A rocket paced horror story. I enjoyed the hell out of this book." Shotgun Logic Reviews

C.G. Mosley
BAKER COUNTY
BIGFOOT CHRONICLE

Marie Bledsoe only wants her missing brother Kurt back. She'll stop at nothing to make it happen and, with the help of Kurt's friend Tony, along with Sheriff Ray Cochran, Marie embarks on a terrifying journey deep into the belly of the mysterious Walker Laboratory to find him. However, what she and her companions find lurking in the laboratory basement is beyond comprehension. There are cryptids from the forest being held captive there and something...else. Enjoy this suspenseful tale from the mind of C.G. Mosley, author of Wood Ape. Welcome back to Baker County, a place where monsters do lurk in the night!

Check out other great

Cryptid Novels!

Ian Faulkner

CRYPTID

Be careful what you look for. You might just find it.1996. A group of 14 students walked into the trackless virgin forests of Graham Island, British Columbia for a three-day hike. They were never seen again. 2019. An American TV crew retrace those students' steps to attempt to solve a 23-year-old mystery.A disparate collection of characters arrives on the island. But all is not as it seems. Two of them carry dark secrets. Terrible knowledge that will mean death for some – but a fighting chance of survival for others. In the hidden depths of the forests – man is on the menu. Some mysteries should remain unsolved...

Eric S. Brown

LOCH NESS HORROR

The Order of the Eternal Light, a secret organization have foretold the end of the human race. In order to save all humanity, agents of the Order must locate the Loch Ness Monster and obtain a sample of its blood for within in it is the key to stopping the apocalypse but finding the monster will be no easy task.

Check out other great

Cryptid Novels!

Edward J. McFadden III

THE CRYPTID CLUB

When cryptozoologist Ash Cohn receives a gold embossed printed invitation inviting him to join The Cryptid Club, he sees the resolution to all his problems.Famous cryptid scientist and biologist, Lester Treemont, one of the world's richest men, and the leader of the Cryptid Club, is dying. What he offers via his invitation is a chance to succeed him. To take over his wealth, laboratory, and discoveries. All Ash has to do is beat eight others like him in a series of tests both mental and physical involving Treemont's collection of cryptids. Seems simple enough, and Ash has nothing to lose.Nine strangers from across the globe, all with reasons for wanting to win. When they start dying one by one, the competition shifts to one of survival. Who among them will rise to the top and reign over The Cryptid Club?

William Meikle

INFESTATION

It was supposed to be a simple mission. A suspected Russian spy boat is in trouble in Canadian waters. Investigate and report are the orders. But when Captain John Banks and his squad arrive, it is to find an empty vessel, and a scene of bloody mayhem. Soon they are in a fight for their lives, for there are things in the icy seas off Baffin Island, scuttling, hungry things with a taste for human flesh. They are swarming. And they are growing. "Scotland's best Horror writer" - Ginger Nuts of Horror "The premier storyteller of our time." - Famous Monsters of Filmland